THE WHITE LINE

The white line separates the sterile sanctuary of the surgeon from the rest of the world. When lovely Nurse Susan Farley stepped across that line, green-gowned and capped, she was no longer a woman, but a highly trained robot responding to the sharp commands of Dr. Arch Curtis, surgeon.

But one day, the operation completed, Susan crossed back over the white line to the everyday world. As she was pulling off her mask, she felt a pair of strong hands on her shoulders. Dr. Arch Curtis was drawing her to him, his harsh voice gentle with concern for her.

Susan's heart leaped with happiness. Was it possible this dedicated man wanted her to share his whole life, his life on both sides of the line?

NURSE FARLEY'S DECISION

by Teresa Holloway

BANTAM BOOKS  NEW YORK

*This low-priced Bantam Book
has been completely reset in a type face
designed for easy reading, and was
printed from new plates. It contains the complete
text of the original hard-cover edition.*
NOT ONE WORD HAS BEEN OMITTED

NURSE FARLEY'S DECISION

*A Bantam Book / published by arrangement with
Thomas Bouregy and Company*

PRINTING HISTORY

*Bouregy edition published December 1959
Bantam edition published August 1961*

Bantam Books are published by Bantam Books, Inc. Its trade-mark, consisting of the words "Bantam Books" and the portrayal of a bantam, is registered in the United States Patent Office and in other countries. Marca Registrada. Printed in the United States of America. Bantam Books, Inc., 271 Madison Ave., New York 16, N. Y.

To my beloved mother, whose courageous recovery, in St. Vincent's Hospital in Jacksonville, Florida, from a "compound, comminuted fracture of the left humerus," gave me the background for this novel.

CHAPTER 1

In the predawn quiet, the great hospital slept. The public-address system had hushed its incessant summons for disembodied names; the corridors were empty, darkened caverns. Susan Farley, in her newly acquired nurse's cap and immaculate white uniform, stood in the doorway of her father's room.

It seemed to her that the hands on the big wall clock, in the island of light surrounding the desk of the Night Supervisor, stood still, while her own sense of time raced within her.

Where was the orderly she had sent for the refill of the life-giving glucose? The doctor had been very explicit in his orders that the patient have continuous intravenous feeding until all danger of post-operative shock was past. The rasping, shallow breathing in the dimness of the room behind her told Susan's trained ear that her father was not yet beyond that danger point. She went back to the bedside on noiseless feet.

I could have gotten it myself twice, by now, Susan thought, then made a conscious effort at control. No wonder the Administrator of Nursing Services frowned on assigning graduate nurses to care for members of their own families. Susan was learning, the hard way, what it meant to be objective. She held her wrist under the cone of light from the night lamp. Only ten minutes?

At last! No—the white-clad figure at the door was Mrs. O'Neill, the Night Supervisor. Susan joined her, and they moved away from the open door together.

"How is he?" the older nurse asked, managing to convey something of her sympathy for Susan in her whisper.

"About the same. I think his pulse is stronger, but the blood pressure is up only two points since the last I.V." Susan wasn't going to let this experienced nurse see that her heart was racing with fear. Maybe she'd have been less frightened if her father's surgery had been for anything but cancer of the lung. Her mother had died of the same thing four years ago.

"This next pint will bring it up," Mrs. O'Neill assured her. "It's too bad, your first case after graduation being so serious and so personal. Are you going to do private duty right along?"

Susan knew that this was an effort to distract her from the passage of time, a kindly gesture on the part of O'Neill. A lump in Susan's throat prevented her from answering; she shook her head, the tears in her blue eyes sparkling in the light from the end of the hall, but not overflowing. She drew a long breath that wasn't entirely steady, before she said, "I wanted very much to do operating room technique. Dr. Curtis thinks there is a need for nurses specializing in cancer surgery."

"Dr. Curtis is a fine doctor." A call light went on down the hall, and Mrs. O'Neill turned away with a lift of one hand that Susan knew was a rare gesture from the senior nurse.

It seemed almost as if Susan's thoughts had summoned Dr. Curtis, for his long stride brought him toward Room 418 two steps ahead of the orderly with the requisitioned supplies.

"Thought you might like a little company," the young surgeon said in the deep voice that Susan had come to know, and respond to, during her months of training at St. Patrick's.

"Bless you, Arch." Her throat felt the stricture of tears again, but this time they didn't reach her eyes. Her nails bit sharply into her palms in her effort to be calm.

Dr. Curtis was listening to his patient's heartbeat.

If he heard mine, he'd take me off the case, Susan thought, watching the dark head bent over the gray one. She pulled her eyes away, and with gentle sureness, checked the plastic tubing that reached from the inverted jar to her father's wrist. The adhesive held the feeder needle firmly in the fragile flesh, injecting the fluid a drop at a time. She adjusted the board to which his arm was strapped, and felt his feet beneath the cover to see if they were warmer. She thought they were.

"He'll do," Arch Curtis was saying. "This isn't uncommon after lung surgery, you know. You'll be surprised how quickly he'll come out of this now." Even in the dimness, Susan could see the kindness in the brown eyes that regarded her from the other side of the hospital bed. "Time for a coffee break," he told her firmly.

"But I can't leave now," she objected.

"We'll see about that." He left the room, and a moment later returned with an aide. He picked up a chair and placed it in the doorway. "Sit here, will you?" The aide sat, and with a final glance toward the elevated bottle on the stand by the bed, Susan followed the tall young resident down the hall.

Neither spoke until they were in the elevator. When its sliding door had sighed shut behind them, Arch Curtis put his hand under her chin and raised her face. "Circles under blue eyes are danger signals," he diagnosed. "Rest is indicated."

"I'm fine," Susan assured him. "I'll rest when he's better."

"Why don't you go home and let someone else relieve you?" The elevator stopped at the first floor and the automatic doors slid open. "While your father's under sedation, he needs someone to sit with him, not to nurse. You know that."

"Arch–" Susan took the cup of coffee he brought, put her elbows on the bare table top and for a brief moment rested her aching head on her hands. The big cafeteria was deserted except for a scattering of duty nurses at the other end of the long room, and the intermittent comings and goings of the counter crew readying the place for the breakfast rush a few hours away.

"Yeah? Drink your coffee." It was like Dr. Arch Curtis to know that sympathy would bring the ready tears just under the surface.

"Dad's illness is going to cost us more money than the Farleys have," Susan said. "Of course now that I'm capped, I'll be making money right along. But it will take a lot to see that Grace finishes college."

"Does Grace have to finish college?" The brown eyes were noncommittal now.

"Well, you know Dad had his heart set on my being a teacher–and for me to quit after only one year on the campus was a bitter blow to him. So it's doubly important for Grace to get her degree." Susan spread her fingers around the cup, warming them. She shivered in the air-conditioned chill of the cafeteria.

"She could get her education after she makes the money to pay for it," Arch said reasonably.

"We've been over all that at home." Susan's voice was husky with tiredness. "I pulled out of the family pattern to be able to do something about this cancer horror, when mother died, and I owe Dad and Grace something for making it possible for me to train at St. Patrick's. If Dad can go back to teaching, maybe it will all work out. Otherwise," she took a deep swallow of the hot coffee, "I'll have to take Dr. Mitchell's offer to be his office nurse."

The young resident's big fist hit the table in a bang that made the saucers jump. The people at the other end of the room looked at them curiously. "No!" he said.

"The salary would be twice as much—"

"But you'd be going back on the very thing for which you left college. Do you think you can contribute anything to the cancer movement by soothing the ruffled feathers of Dr. Mitchell's society practice?" He lighted a cigarette with fingers that shook.

"Well, he does have some patients who come to him for skin cancer work . . ." Susan knew her defense was weak.

"So he does. We won't go into his skin cancer work; we've been there before. Doesn't it make you feel anything to see a man with the talents our Chief of Staff has doing cosmetic plastic surgery? You want to dedicate yourself to the eradication of wrinkles and the reshaping of unsightly noses?" Arch didn't wait for an answer, but got up impatiently, picked up the two empty cups and took them over to the counter. "Come on," he said rudely. "That aide can't sit in your father's door forever."

Instead of hurting Susan's feelings, his gruffness gave her the strength to get on her feet and follow him to the elevator. There, he turned and looked searchingly into her eyes. "Go home," he told her, and strode off toward the swinging doors leading to the interns' and residents' quarters.

Wide awake now, Susan went back to Room 418. Her father seemed to be breathing with more depth.

Outside the double windows, the dark was giving way to a deep copper. Susan stood at the window, watching the gold of the dawn play across the surface of the bay. The founders of St. Patrick's had chosen this quiet cove on the outskirts of Palm City—a fast-growing community on Florida's northwest Gulf Coast—for its natural beauty, which was always at its best, Susan felt, at this daybreak hour.

The deeply turfed lawns extended to the bulkhead, ribboned by concrete walkways leading from the various exits to the promenade that ran along the shoreline. Extending for a hundred feet into the bay, halfway between the nurses' dormitories and the hospital, was a covered pier. On good days, the sundeck at the end was always peopled by wheel-chair and ambulatory patients. Now, however, the brisk breeze that bespoke the coming of day rattled the palm fronds and riffled the masses of summer flowers in the border beds. As Susan watched, an electronic finger pressed the button that turned off the lights which at night illuminated the alabaster-white statue of St. Patrick, the hospital's patron saint. The life-sized image, against the unrelieved darkness, was startlingly real, even down to the coiled serpents at the end of his staff. He seemed always to be on the verge of lifting the curved stick and releasing the reptiles into the blossoms at the statue's base. Susan had seen him there in all kinds of weather—hurricanes, squalls, in sheets of rain that swept inland from the roughened bay—and he had become a symbol to her.

"You know I don't want to leave St. Patrick's," she told the statue.

Turning away from the window she began to straighten the disorder of bandage wrappings, discarded newspapers, and crumpled tissues. It was still a mystery to her how a room whose chief occupant was bedridden could be so littered. Then she eased her tired body into the plastic chair. *I'd never call this an easy chair*, she thought, *but I'd better get out of it if I'm to stay awake*. She got up an inch at a time, to keep the plastic upholstery from crackling, and drew a straight chair over to the side of the bed.

Poor lamb, she thought, the lump in her throat threatening again. *He hasn't been the same since Mother went.* She wished she had some way of letting him know that she understood his preference for Grace; that she knew he had found comfort in her younger sister's high-spirited temperament. He looked waxlike, lying there on his back, his prominent, aristocratic nose seeming to dominate his whole face.

"Susan?" her father said in a voice that was dry and cracked.

"I'm here, dear." She put her cheek on one of the thin hands, the one without the needle.

"I dreamed you were dead," the dry voice said. "Grace made the dean's list, dearest; she's going to be a fine teacher."

Susan's heart sank. It was her mother to whom he had spoken. That other Susan, the dearer one. *Grace is dearer, too, and I can come along if I like*, Susan thought bitterly. For a frozen moment, she was tempted to turn down Dr. Mitchell's office position.

She looked around the starkly plastered walls of the hospital room. This was a masonry capsule that shut her and her father away from the rest of the world. The reality of the lusty young town, the traffic lights on Main Street, the causeways to the island beaches and the main highway bridge to the south of town, leading westward to Mobile and New Orleans, these bustling symbols of civilization were the world that would be hers when she was office nurse for Dr. Christopher Mitchell, Chief of Staff at St. Patrick's. It would be goodbye to the gray tiled walls of Surgery, here at the hospital.

Maybe, considering the hostile attitude of Dr. Arch Curtis, it would be goodbye to the warmth of their friendship that had deepened into something very close to love. *I might as well face it,* Susan thought.

Arch was wrapped up in the hospital. And she wanted it that way. This huge E-shaped brick building was the core of Archibald Curtis' existence; if she were a part of it, she would grow closer to him. Otherwise, he'd think of her when he wasn't immersed in that anesthesia-saturated atmosphere of the operating table. He'd think of her often at first, and then only at intervals.

But Grace must be taught to be a good teacher. Susan's full, soft lips firmed to a thin line.

CHAPTER II

Amy Stapleton, Susan's roommate during her last year in training, relieved Susan so that she could go home for a few hours. She reached home before Grace left for the campus.

"I was afraid you'd be too late to tell me how Dad is," her sister greeted her.

"Better. His blood pressure's up ten points." Susan poured herself a cup of coffee and put bread into the toaster. She was too tired to take any other steps toward breakfast. She slid into the breakfast-alcove seat and leaned her head against its high back. She was almost asleep, sitting there, when the pop-up toaster brought her back to her surroundings.

"Who's with him now?" Grace was applying a bluish-red lipstick to her curving lips. It was a shade that would have destroyed Susan's pastel claim to beauty, but it went well with the dramatic white-petal skin and sooty hair of her younger sister.

"Amy. She's taking a few weeks between graduation and duty, so she was free to help out. I don't know what I'd have done, otherwise. I guess the floor nurses could cope, but Dad's pretty sick for that just now." Susan looked for the butter dish, saw that it wasn't on the table, and decided it wasn't worth the effort of getting up for it.

"I guess you mean that for a crack about my not cutting classes. Dad wouldn't want me to cut." Grace helped herself to a second cup of coffee, and was about to drink it, standing up.

"Sit down, Grace. I must talk to you." Susan dragged herself up out of the half-sleep that fogged her brain.

"I'll be late," Grace began. But she smoothed her linen sheath carefully to preserve it against wrinkling and sat gingerly on the painted seat across from Susan.

"Have another piece of toast?" Susan pushed down the toaster rack.

"I'll be fat if I do; I didn't have the first one." Grace

drew her compact out of her clutch purse and regarded an all-but-invisible spot on her chin. "What in the world am I going to do about my complexion?" she mourned. "Jimmy hates pimply girls, and he's taking me to the Seminole Club tomorrow night. What did you want to say, Susan?"

Susan sighed. What was the use of spoiling things for Grace? It wouldn't even sink in, telling her what a sacrifice it would be to do office duty. But on the other hand, it wasn't fair to the younger girl not to give her a chance to carry her share of the load.

"Honey, you know this illness is going to make Dad feel pretty washed out for a long time," she began.

"I've cried a river over it—you know that," Grace protested.

"Yes, baby, I know. But tears won't get us out of our troubles. I mean, Dad may not be well enough to go back to the classroom in September. And we might as well face it—it will be five years before we're sure. He may never go back."

"Are you trying to frighten me?" Grace's enormous brown eyes opened to their fullest. "I don't think that's fair, when I've got an extra hard physics test today. Dad's strong; he's going to be all right." She snapped her compact shut with decision. "I've got to go now."

Susan watched her sister get up in one lithe movement and smooth down her snug dress with graceful, long-fingered hands. Hands, Susan couldn't help thinking, that had never held a bedpan or given a bath to a helpless person whose dead weight was almost impossible to shift. But she let Grace go without further talk, picked up her dishes and rinsed them under the hot-water faucet. They were hardly dry in the rack before Susan was in bed, sleep smothering her like a dark blanket.

It took all her will-power to be back at the hospital by noon.

"He's fine," Amy greeted her when she pushed open the door to Room 418. Susan smiled at her friend's obvious pride in the progress of her patient, and looked at her father anxiously. He was asleep, and breathing deeply.

"Come outside for a minute." Amy gathered her things together and Susan followed her to the sun porch, a few feet from the door of 418.

"Dr. Mitchell was in to see you," Amy began. "If I had

a chance to work for anyone as handsome as he is, I'd forsake private duty in a flash."

"Did he say what he wanted?"

"He said to come by to see him this afternoon."

"Well, when Grace comes, maybe." Susan sounded doubtful. She kept watching for the light to go on over her father's door.

"What's the matter with you, Sue? I can't see why anyone wouldn't jump at the chance to work with Dr. Mitchell. He's a wonderful plastic surgeon, besides being Chief of Staff at St. Patrick's; he can afford to pay you a big salary. And he's as charming a man as I ever saw."

"I know," Susan answered slowly. "But I want to learn all I can about cancer. Because it's a medical problem, the biggest we have, people need to know about the medical advances and limitations. And because a nurse is so often consulted by people seeking information in terms he can understand, I want to be able to share my knowledge. I only know enough now to realize I know practically nothing."

"The Chief's back," Amy said.

Susan turned and watched St. Patrick's Chief of Staff come down the corridor, with the Floor Supervisor a respectful two paces behind him. He paused at her father's door, but caught sight of her before his outstretched hand could shove it inward.

"Oh, Miss Farley." His distinguished face was lighted by his most gracious smile. The lapel of his blue gabardine suit held a tiny sweetheart rosebud, and Susan realized that she'd never seen him without a flower there.

Except when he's in Surgery, and even in his green surgery outfit he manages to look dapper and polished, she thought. Personally, she preferred the hit-and-miss way Arch Curtis wore his clothes. Somehow they gave the effect of being invited to go along wherever Arch might be going, as an afterthought.

"I see by your father's chart that he's better today." Dr. Mitchell nodded to the nurse who was with him, and she walked away.

"Yes, Doctor," Susan murmured, hoping that her face showed nothing of her rebellion against the high-handed attitude Dr. Mitchell adopted, and the staff bowed to.

"I was by earlier, to tell you that Miss Dodge is leaving a week earlier than she had planned. It will leave me shorthanded."

"Miss Stapleton was just telling me that I missed seeing you."

"Could you come on Monday?" The charm was flashed on again.

"If my father—"

"Oh, I'll see that a nurse from the registry handles that for you." Dr. Mitchell's well-manicured hand brushed away the obstacle of special nurses, their scarcity and their costliness.

"Stop being a dog in the manger," Susan admonished herself. "Thank you, Doctor." She gave him her nicest smile, to make up for her lack of gratitude.

The public-address system broke into speech. "All doctors report to Emergency," the impersonal voice said crisply. "All doctors in the house report to Emergency." Susan and Amy looked at each other with alarm. Dr. Mitchell seemed annoyed.

"What *now!*" he said impatiently. But he didn't hesitate. His graceful walk was still smooth, but he covered the ground. He was gone around the L at the end of the corridor in seconds.

Amy followed close on his heels. If all the doctors were needed, all the nurses would be, too.

That's the trouble with this air-conditioned isolation we live in, Susan thought. *In the old days, we'd have heard ambulances screaming up to the west entrance. These things burst out at us from a box on the wall.* The light went on over her father's door, and she went toward Room 418 rather than to the desk for information.

"Good morning, dear," her father greeted her.

"Good afternoon, Dad." Susan bent over and kissed the pale cheek.

"Afternoon?" As weak as he was, his face lighted up. "Then Grace should soon be here."

"In not so long," Susan said cheerfully. She put her foot on the pedal that lowered the head of the bed. This was what John Farley had wanted when he pulled the call light. Susan felt encouraged that he cared whether his head was too high or too low.

There was a brisk knock on the ground glass of the door, and Arch Curtis came in before Susan could answer it.

"Mr. Farley, we're going to borrow your competent daughter for awhile, if you don't mind," he said, without the slightest hint in his voice of the emergency downstairs. "The floor nurses will look after you; just pull on your light if you want anything." He felt the sick man's pulse.

Susan said nothing. She used the brief moments to pick up her case holding fountain pen and thermometer. She knew without being told that Surgery would be filling up. Whether she would be needed there, or to relieve a supervisor, she'd be prepared.

"We've phoned Mrs. O'Neill to report; she'll know what to do for your father." Arch was walking faster on the highly polished floor and Susan could barely keep up with him.

"What's *happened?*" she asked breathlessly. He held a thumb on the elevator button to make sure the automatic car stopped for them. Sometimes it didn't.

"A sailor going a hundred miles an hour hit a school bus. An early bus." There was a white rim around the finely chiseled edges of the young doctor's generous mouth.

"Dear God!" Susan's breath was a prayer. An early bus—that meant little children.

"Where?" They got on the elevator. Its flight up the single floor to where most orthopedic surgery was done seemed interminable.

"On the highway bridge. Come on." Taking her elbow, he almost propelled her toward the leather-covered doors under the sign marked "Surgery."

He pushed her over the white line, with its legend painted on the tile floor: "Don't come beyond this line unless in surgical gown."

"Come on, scrub." He flung an order at an intern near the door of the linen closet. "Bring gown and headgear to Miss Farley." He himself was up to his elbows under the faucets that were turned on and off with a foot pedal. The smell of antiseptic soap enveloped them both. People in the faded green of surgery clothes were coming and going in quiet haste, past the hall door.

"How many?" Susan asked. She was ready, though she had no idea what awaited her.

"Twenty-two here, others at Presbyterian Memorial. Dr. Mitchell is in there." Arch moved his head toward the largest operating room. "He's already sent down two of them."

Susan marveled. It had been only minutes since the first call had sounded over the loud-speaker. It was this ability to act well under pressure that had earned Christopher Mitchell his place as Chief of Staff in the largest hospital on Florida's northwest coast.

Why had Arch taken the time to come for her, instead of sending someone? She had no time to ask him. He was running a tentative hand over the chest and ribs of a boy who seemed to Susan to be all skin and bones.

The anesthetist was busy with the rack that was kept in readiness with the various types of gases and chemicals used in the complex world of modern anesthesia. Susan was aware of the cone being fitted over the small, bloody face as she slapped the instruments into Arch's waiting hand in response to his commands. The sweat on his broad forehead was wiped off frequently by another nurse. Not Amy. Susan thought this one a student. Then she didn't think any more, just obeyed the deep voice that came to her out of the haze of fatigue and sorrow that was engulfing her.

She hardly realized when one small body was replaced by another, and then another. It was all a confusion of broken arms, legs, hips, ribs . . . "Dear God . . ." She repeated her earlier prayer, over and over. It was somehow worse because these were hardly more than babies. And there were more downstairs, on the fourth floor, ordinarily used for abdominal surgery, the cancer work of Arch or Dr. Mitchell, in fact, almost all the major surgery here except obstetrics and orthopedics. There would be ten full operating rooms down there; here there were only four.

Susan closed her mind to the horror of the mental picture. This one was bad enough. To consider them en masse was inconceivable. But she remembered to be thankful that the accident had happened in the afternoon. Earlier in the day, when almost all the doctors did their surgery, there would have been a space problem.

Her hands went on with the endless work required of them. She thought, her eyes aching from the thousands of watts of diffused illumination emanating from the four great circular lighting fixtures, *The world is peopled by animated hands.*

Hands that probe, and set, and sew. Hands that wipe. Hands that hold. Hands that lift.

Years of people's lives went into the training of these hands beneath that brilliant light.

Mothers' lives—teaching gentleness and a desire to serve; fathers' lives, dedicated to earning the money to make knowledge within their grasp; brothers' and sisters' lives, carrying loads heavier than young shoulders should bear, filling in at home to set these hands free to learn.

It was still Arch's voice she heard. But now it was not a

sharp command. It held gentleness. Dully, she realized that the table was empty.

Only Arch's hands now. They were on her shoulders, drawing her gently away.

Susan was surprised to see that it was dark outside.

CHAPTER III

Monday was four days away. Susan didn't need to consult a calendar to know how short was the time. In her mind, she knew she should feel flattered that Dr. Mitchell wanted her. He could have had his choice of the graduating class, almost. Now, however, the others had made their plans, and Susan supposed the rush of sheer circumstance would sweep her into that world of fashionable private practice and fancied ailments.

At least, she thought, cleaning the house with a fervor born of her own unhappiness, *Dad will be coming home soon*. Susan wanted the whole place spotless for the big event. Things would work out. Maybe in a few years, after Grace had her degree, she could go back to St. Patrick's.

"But by then, Arch Curtis won't be there," she told herself. The thought made her stop waxing the kitchen linoleum with the swift long strokes she'd found most effective. Was it to be near the young resident that she was so bent on doing hospital work?

Susan propped her wax-spreader against the range and went over to look in the ancient mirror that hung on the back of the pantry door. The girl she saw there had hair that was deeply red, its soft waves close to her head; and when she turned to survey herself critically, the heavy chignon at the base of her slender neck came into view. Should she cut her hair? Would Arch like it better that way? She might as well admit it—the thought of the rangy, black-haired resident added an undertone of excitement and meaning to life. Susan's blue eyes widened at her own reflection. "That's just fine. To fall in love at a time like this—when neither of us has time for love. And he certainly hasn't said anything about loving you," she told the girl in the mirror.

Susan wanted to sit down at the breakfast table and dream about Arch for a few minutes. But characteristically, she finished the kitchen floor. She had to go to the dentist. And besides, it would be better to make herself think of

Arch in the old, uncluttered way, until he himself changed the color of their relationship.

She showered and dressed, choosing a yellow shirtwaist dress with rolled-up sleeves, easing it down over her shoulders so as not to disarrange her hair. Susan didn't wear hats. Few girls in Palm City did.

She was anxious to get all her chores out of the way before going to work steadily. And this annual trip to the dentist she regarded as one of the most irksome. She sat in the waiting room and leafed through several of the worn magazines. No one else was here, and she knew the view from the window by heart. Only the difference in the year's models of the parked cars in the lot across the street marked this visit from those of the last ten years that she could remember. It was about time for her appointment. She looked impatiently at her watch.

The elevator down the hall clanged open—even the sound of the old wrought-iron doors was the same. High heels clicked toward this office, at the end of the corridor. Susan entertained herself by visualizing the type of person who would walk like that. Short steps—short stature. Probably slightly overweight, for there was a sound of heft to the way the feet met the tiled floor. Then the door opened.

Susan gasped, but made herself look again at the neglected magazine in her lap. The newcomer was short, as she had thought; she was also decidedly on the plump side. Once she had been pretty, in a soft, round way. Her hair was bleached, and the gentle blue eyes had a defensive, pleading look, even in their brief meeting with Susan's. It was the woman's mouth that was grotesque. Against the pink and white complexion, the bottom lip was drawn down into a quarter-sized bleached circle that Susan's trained eye knew to be a radium burn. The smile that the woman directed toward Susan was enough to evoke tears in the eyes of the beholder.

"Have we long to wait?" the woman asked, seating herself with her back to the open window's merciless light.

"I'm about due in." Susan made her reply matter-of-fact. She was thinking, *Poor thing, her prettiness was probably the dominant factor in her life. Now that that's gone, she has lost the incentive for trimness and everything else.* Susan wondered if she would ever be completely professional in her own attitude toward the human misery around her. She doubted it.

The other patient hunted in her purse, brought out a battered package of cigarettes and offered one to Susan. To Susan's refusal, the woman nodded approvingly.

"I'm the last one who should smoke, I guess," she said. "But what difference does it make now?" This seemed to be addressed more to herself than to Susan. But not wanting to appear unsympathetic, Susan answered her.

"A person can't always do what's best for them," she said comfortingly. "I never seemed to have time for smoking, myself, so I didn't take it up."

"I'd be a different woman if *I* hadn't." The woman's voice was well modulated; it was obvious that she was educated, but her clothes were cheap and not even clean.

"A nurse hasn't the opportunity for personal indulgence that people in other work have," Susan thought aloud. "I felt that I'd have to choose between being considerate of my patients or indulgent of myself. So I never took it up." She glanced again at her watch. The doctor must be involved in something unusually time-consuming this morning. She wished he'd hurry; she had so very much to do before Monday.

"Oh, you're a nurse?" There was a note of quickened interest in the woman's voice.

"I've been a registered nurse for two weeks." Susan smiled at the pride in her own voice.

"What kind of nursing will you go into?" The faded blue eyes were almost smiling back, although the disfigured mouth moved with difficulty in the effort of forming the words.

"I'm—going to work for Dr. Christopher Mitchell . . . as his office nurse."

The effect on the other woman was astonishing. She drew up her short figure to its fullest sitting height, and put her plump feet primly together. As nearly as was possible, she compressed her lips. The plucked brows came together, and the blue eyes hardened. "Oh," she said in a tone of finality. Its unmistakable coolness put a period to any further talk.

Susan was glad when the dentist put his head into the waiting room to say he was ready for her.

Dr. Thomas had been the family dentist all Susan's life. He'd extracted her baby teeth, and Grace's. He was their father's firm friend. Susan was always glad of an opportunity to visit with him.

"How are you, Susan?" The wrinkles around the spectacled eyes deepened with a smile of welcome as he buckled the towel around her neck.

"Fine, except of course tired after all this worry about Dad," she said. "And from rushing around trying to get ready for work next Monday. You know I'm going to work for Dr. Mitchell?" She opened her mouth for Dr. Thomas' exploring probes.

"Oh?" The old dentist sounded remote. Susan opened her eyes and raised her brows. When there was a chance, she spoke defensively.

"That's the second time this morning I've had that reply to the same statement," she said. "The woman in your waiting room put me in a definite deep freeze when I said I was going to work for Dr. Mitchell."

"Yes. Well," the dentist resumed his search for possible cavities, "perhaps she had reason. Though it's not for me to say." He turned around and began to assemble the materials for the cleaning process Susan always dreaded.

"Dr. Thomas, you know you aren't going to leave me in that kind of uncertainty." Susan sat up straight. "Right now it's important for me to know these things. What has she got against Dr. Mitchell?"

"She had a rough spot on her lip, and he thought it would be well to remove it with radiation," Dr. Thomas said in a colorless tone. "Maybe it was malignant—it could have been, though there was no biopsy. Even so, the burn was pretty drastic. As you see. And it seems it was necessary to go back again and again. Her husband had a sort of semi-executive job at the bank—well . . . the thing eventually took all their savings. Unfortunately," Dr. Thomas cleared his throat, "the husband went off with another woman. My patient finds it difficult to make ends meet. She thinks she's too ugly to work in public. She does hand ironing in a laundry that specializes in that sort of work. . . . How's Grace these days?"

Susan knew the subject of the woman in the waiting room was closed. But it left a nagging ache in her mind, and when Dr. Thomas let her out the hall door without going back through the reception room, she resolved to talk to Arch about it. Wouldn't skin grafting alleviate that ugly scar?

All the way home, Susan thought how a scar on a person's body could make a scar on his soul. But she made up her mind not to be hasty in her judgment of Dr. Chris. There were always two sides—her father's favorite philosophy.

She didn't see Arch until Friday night. He called up to say that he had some free time, and could she go for a ride. She told him she'd be delighted.

When she dropped a teacup, breaking it into dozens of pieces, and spilled hand lotion on the glass top of her dresser, Grace looked cynical.

"Fancy Miss Calm herself having the shakes," she remarked. Grace was giving herself a home permanent, and the house was redolent with the smell of wave solution.

"It's that awful odor," Susan countered. "Couldn't you do that some other time?"

"I had to pick a night when I didn't have a date. If I didn't do it now, no one would ask me any more. You're smug because your hair is naturally wavy. If you and Arch come back early enough, I'll make you some cookies. They'll be mix, but he won't mind, eating that old institution food all the time." Grace rolled a long lock of black hair onto the curler.

"Thanks, honey. We just may do that."

Susan heard Arch pull into the oyster-shell driveway. The Farley bungalow was in the older section of town. Older by Palm City standards; the community had been a seafood town before the first Florida land boom. In those days, there had been only a few wood houses on the bayfront. Then, after the speculation frenzy of 1926 receded, there was a rash of pseudo-Spanish stucco bungalows. Professor Farley had brought his bride to one of these, located near the campus of Palm City Junior College. A succession of hurricanes had taken their toll of the tarpaper-and-gravel roof, of the skimpy stucco over the wood-lath construction, but patchwork repair kept the weather out, and Susan kept the house clean. She wasn't ashamed of its defects, but she'd just as soon Arch didn't come into the prevailing odor at the moment. So she met him at the steps.

"Hi, Nurse Farley." Arch was as tall as she was, standing on the second step from the ground.

"Hi." Susan felt shy. Though there never seemed to be enough time to talk about all the thousands of things that needed saying, right now she couldn't think of a single thing to say.

Arch misunderstood her silence. "Susan," he began as soon as the car was cruising along the bayfront drive, "Mrs. Branch said to tell you she wasn't going to close her staff recruitment until you were sure you weren't going to be with us."

"I'm too sure," Susan said gloomily. "Where are we going?" She'd rather not talk shop tonight. What could she say that hadn't already been said?

"I thought you might like to stop by the hospital for a minute to see your father. I've got a pop call to make myself. How about it?"

"Fine." But Susan knew a sense of disappointment.

"I'll come up after you when I'm through," Arch promised. "Say!" She was on her way to the elevator when his call stopped her. She turned around. Arch came up to her with that sort of loping walk that was so much a part of him. "I meant to tell you. Your hair looks like a coal fire on a cold night," he told her gravely. "All flaming and dark at the same time. It's the darnedest effect I ever saw. See you later."

Susan walked on air all the way to Room 418.

She found her father sitting in the big plastic chair.

"Aren't you the smart one," she greeted him. Her kiss on his cheek found it still feverish, however.

"I'd been hoping you'd come," John Farley told her.

Susan felt a sting of self-reproach. She wouldn't have come tonight if Arch hadn't had to be here. And her father seemed very fragile, sitting there in a robe that was too big for him.

"I've been doing a lot of thinking," he went on gravely, "ever since Dr. Curtis came up for you that night after the school-bus accident." The whole town had been shocked over that disaster; its senseless tragedy had saddened her father, Susan knew. But she had a feeling that it wasn't about the accident he wished to speak. She sat down on the hassock by his slim, slippered feet, and watched him with anxiety. Was he overtaxing himself?

"I've felt very close to your mother, these days in the hospital." Susan nodded understandingly. "Perhaps in wanting you to be a really fine schoolteacher, your mother and I were selfishly trying to push you into the profession we ourselves loved. I'm sure if she'd known that you would prefer nursing, she would have sensed that you'd contribute just as much to the world in that capacity as we wanted you to in the classroom."

Susan glowed. Her father's understanding meant more to her than anything in the world. She reached for his hand, and he took hers in both of his. He went on talking, after an emotion-filled moment.

"It came over me that if you were good enough for them

to come up here after you, sending someone not so skilled to look after this old crock," he took one thin hand and made a fist of it, "you certainly must have made a mark in your surgical studies."

"Yes, sir," Susan murmured, unable to say more.

"So I sent for young Curtis. I asked him point-blank about this office job. He said it was a waste. That any good R.N. could do that, but only someone with your God-given gift for operating-room technique could have done what you did during that awful afternoon and night." Her father paused, seeming to need energy to go on.

"We are going to make other arrangements. You worked to get your training, doing without any of the luxuries and frivolities a young girl craves. Grace can do the same to get her teaching degree. We'll both help her all we can—and I'm sure I have some connections that can help find a scholarship lying around somewhere. In any event, you call your stylish doctor friend and tell him to find himself another girl." The brown eyes that were so like Grace's were twinkling now, even though the pale lips drooped with fatigue.

Susan tasted the salt of tears as she put both arms around her father. She all but lifted him in her strong grasp, helping him back to bed.

She'd have something to tell Arch now! No danger of being tongue-tied when she was alone with him . . .

Her mind stopped its racing in happy circles. Of course! Arch had known all the time—that was why he'd phoned her, and brought her here. He hadn't wanted a date, after all.

CHAPTER IV

The damp wind that blustered and shouldered its way along the concrete driveway that curved into the main entrance of St. Patrick's and back onto the street rattled the skirt of Susan's starched uniform, and she hurried her steps to get inside before the rain came. When the sky was this leaden, scudding gray, rain was imminent. Grace had taken Susan's raincoat from its accustomed place on the back seat.

She almost collided with Maggie Branch, St. Patrick's Director of Nursing Services. As a student nurse, Susan had always found Mrs. Branch strict but just. She had thought the other girls' attitude, that the Director was a human machine, unjustified and unfair. Susan was glad to see "Ma Maggie," as the undergraduate nurses called the Director behind her stiffly erect back.

"Mrs. Branch, I was on my way to see you." Susan's blue eyes were dark with happiness in what she called her "release from bondage."

"Oh?" The older woman's features remained unrelaxed.

Susan felt dashed for a moment. But that was foolish. Ma Maggie always preserved an attitude of dignity, and after all, Susan had come breezing through the big revolving front door like a tornado. The Director would think her lacking in professional poise. Susan's dimple showed briefly in her left cheek. She wanted to take the unyielding lady-ramrod standing there before her, and whirl her around and around. It was heavenly, knowing she would be a part of the hospital world from now on.

"If you're going to be in your office, could I come by and arrange for assignment to Operating Room?" Susan's question was merely a matter of formality. She would make the appointment, but the staggering shortage of nursing help made it a foregone conclusion that there would be room for her. Besides, hadn't Mrs. Branch sent her word that she would hold a place for her?

"Certainly come by, Farley." The older woman's expression remained granitelike. "However, I believe that slot is already staffed." She went on out the door. Susan stood stunned.

Yesterday she had telephoned Dr. Mitchell that her father had expressed a desire to have her remain on duty at St. Patrick's. She had apologized, and offered to come to his office to work until he could find another nurse.

He had been, Susan thought, a bit formal, but this could have been because he had someone in his office at the time. And he'd turned down her offer to fill in, assuring her smoothly that he could manage nicely.

Susan walked to the elevator in an unbelieving daze. She waited for the car to settle on the main floor, not seeing anything of the bustle that meant the three o'clock shift was breaking.

A woman who had been a patient for several months rolled herself past in a wheel chair, and Susan answered her greeting without realizing who had spoken until a long time later, when the painful events of this nightmare afternoon were to retrace themselves across her memory.

The elevator came, and Susan put a finger on the button numbered "four." The finger she saw as if it belonged to someone else—a straight index finger of the right hand, terminating in an unlacquered nail. There were three small freckles on the second joint. Hand lotions were no good for them. A small girl's allowance could buy a lot of different brands, over the years. The car doors slid open, the light above them going on behind the fourth numeral.

Susan's white pumps, sensibly heeled and soled in rubber, took her down the long corridor to Room 418. Her father was asleep. She retraced her steps to the desk. It was empty, but she hoped that Mrs. O'Neill was on duty. Then she saw that the floor nurses were bunched into the doorway of the floor kitchen, and beyond. O'Neill was briefing them on the status of cases on Four, East.

"The appendectomy in oh-seven gets penicillin hypos every four hours; the goiter in eleven has changed sedation; if the gallbladder in twenty-one needs lab work, see to it and then notify Dr. Mitchell . . ." Leslie O'Neill checked each chart as she spoke, handing them to an aide to be replaced on their hooks behind the desk. She'd acknowledged Susan's presence by a nod; Susan knew this few minutes was one of the most important intervals of the day in the routine of the busy surgical hall.

She stood aside as the younger girls in their crisp white

dresses dispersed from the briefing and went about their tasks. O'Neill sat down in the chair behind the desk and sighed with fatigue. The oncoming Supervisor had been called off the hall for a few minutes, and O'Neill explained that she was hanging around until her relief got back.

"They look younger than we ever did," Susan remarked, watching the several nurses and the aides scatter.

"I thought that about your class," Mrs. O'Neill remarked. "My outfit trained in blue-and-white striped uniforms, with heavy starched collars and cuffs. A white turn-out in those days meant something more than a girl from the Hospitality Shop downstairs; we didn't get white uniforms until we were capped."

"Well, this is a day of uniforms, I guess," Susan remarked, keeping the conversation on the surface because one of the students was still in the kitchen. "Even the auxiliary has its special uniform—and very cute it is, too."

"Those pink pinafores and the crisp blouses are probably one of the real reasons why our society set does so nobly," Leslie O'Neill said. "If that sounds catty, it's because I've had a hard day, and one of the Pink Ladies was sassy to one of the orderlies, and he quit."

"Oh, no!" A good orderly was as hard to come by as a good nurse.

"He left the elevator door open, and the Pink One had to stand on Two, East, with the wagon, for ten minutes. It developed that the door was open because a visitor had fainted at the sight of someone coming down from Surgery on a guerney, complete with I.V. attendant and mouth basin. The latter in use, I take it." O'Neill's tone was dry. She spoke over her shoulder to the nurse in the kitchen. "What are you doing there, Harper?"

"I was hunting the blood pressure sleeve," was the subdued reply.

"It's over on Four, West," Mrs. O'Neill answered. To Susan, she said, "Someday I'm going to work in a hospital where they have adequate equipment. Fancy an installation like St. Patrick's having to lend out the floor's gear." She waited until the student nurse was out of hearing. Then she turned to Susan with a listening look.

"Do you know why Ma Maggie turned me down for O.R. duty?" Susan's face was bleak.

"Don't talk so loud," O'Neill cautioned. "These walls carry an echo right downtown."

"So they do," Susan replied, understanding beginning to show in her eyes. "Right down to the Medical Arts Building, in fact," she said bitterly.

"I'm going off duty in a minute or two," Mrs. O'Neill reminded her. "Wait for me at the front door, and we can go down to Nick's for coffee. It would be better there than in the cafeteria."

"I'll look in on Dad first," Susan said.

She found her father, comfortably propped up with pillows, reading the newest historical biography, one of a stack of books brought by fellow instructors at the junior college.

"When do you start, dear?" His voice was clearer, firmer.

"Aren't you the smart one?" Susan countered with another question. "And stop sabotaging my few days between the brook and the river. As a matter of fact, I'm making Grace some clothes for her trip to Miami when the session's over," she explained. "I'm going to run down for coffee with Mrs. O'Neill, dear—back in a jiffy." Susan kissed her father and left hurriedly, for fear he might question her further.

After she talked with O'Neill, she decided, she'd try to get in touch with Arch. Did he know about this awful thing that had happened to her? It was one thing to take a job other than her beloved surgery duty because of financial necessity; it was quite another thing—an inconceivable thing—that that duty would be denied her by the hospital authorities.

Of course, O'Neill had meant that Dr. Mitchell had blackballed her. "But it is an almost unwritten law that nurses are assigned to the work they want most to do," she reminded herself. "He couldn't want me badly enough in his old office to lay himself open to the kind of reaction a thing like this is bound to generate among the nursing staff."

Her mind was wrapped up in her problems as she walked slowly to the main stem of the E-shaped building and its battery of elevators. She was almost too engrossed to see Arch Curtis when he rounded the corner of the far wing. The light was to his back. He walked with that litheness that was so much a part of him. In spite of herself, Susan felt her heart give a skip and a hop, as it had been doing lately whenever the young resident with the understanding brown eyes and the lean face was around.

She raised her hand to attract his attention.

He didn't see her. Susan was about to call to him, when a girl with a nimbus of dark curls, cut short so that they looked like a cap of ringlets, and dressed in the pink pinafore of the hospital auxiliary, came swiftly out of the cubbyhole used as a sort of sub-station for gifts and gear from the Hospitality Shop.

That she was delighted to see Arch was immediately and vocally apparent.

"Oh, Doctor, you're just in time!" The girl, piquant and wholly lovely, was exhibiting a shell-like finger that had been pricked and was bleeding. "*Do* come sew me up. I'm sure we'll make a fabulous doctor-patient team," she assured Arch.

I'm sure you will, Susan thought, watching Arch look with a quizzical twinkle at the dainty finger. They turned and went back toward the Dispensary together.

"Down?" A maintenance man opened the elevator door.

"Yes, sir." Susan got on. Down. Down and out. She wouldn't wait for O'Neill. Leaving word with the clerk at the Information desk to tell O'Neill she'd had to go out, and to please notify Fourth, East, that she wouldn't be back to see the patient in Room 418 for awhile, Susan went outdoors. The rain that had threatened earlier in the afternoon was a reality now.

For a moment, she stood on the low steps. She had intended to make her way to the family car and either go home or just drive around. Anywhere. Away from this pile of stone and masonry that she didn't care if she never saw again.

But there was something about the feel of the rain, pelting against her unprotected face and head with needle-like coolness, that changed her direction. Thrusting her hands in her skirt pockets, she raised her chin, straightened her shoulders, and turned toward the bay. She remembered that Arch had once said he'd chosen to intern in St. Patrick's because the bay was "only a thrown milk-bottle's distance" away from it. A few steps now, and Susan's rubber-soled strollers were taking her along the bulkhead.

The wind was rising. The ceiling was almost zero; it was really, she thought, dark enough for the light to go on before the statue of St. Patrick. She walked past it, glaring at the Irish patron for his failure to work out her troubles. She had no idea where she was going. The smell of the sea was coming in with the northeaster; there were seagulls on the railing of the hospital pier. Aimlessly, she turned onto the pier because the gulls were there. Like her, they were solitary, lonely; water was running down their feathers and in a tiny stream off their beaks. The gulls were looking at her with their shoe-button eyes, warily.

"Don't go," she invited them. "There's room for gulls and girls, too, in the rain." Surprisingly, with unblinking regard, they agreed.

"I thought, back there, there was someone out here with you gulls," she told them, walking past in shoes that squished. "I see I was mistaken. Anyway, thanks for not flying away." She supposed her new white strollers were ruined. "You're crazy, walking in the rain in your work clothes. But at least they won't cost like those pointed-toed, needle-heeled things that girl had on. You'd have been scared at those heels, gulls, and my patients would be scared at those inch-long fingernails with that exact shade of pink polish to match the pink pinafore. But wasn't she pretty?"

Susan was nearly to the end of the pier. There was a roof to the pavilion at the T-shaped dockend. "And when you get there, you'll just turn around and come back," she said aloud. "That's the story of the life of Susan Farley, spinster, aged twenty-one."

More to refute her theory that she was getting nowhere than to rest, she sat down on one of the rough board benches. This was where the convalescents always came—and a quiet, unhurried place it was. So remote, today, in the rain. She'd thought there had been someone here, but it was raining hard then, and she guessed the flash of white had been the sea-birds.

"On your feet, Susan," she ordered herself. "You'll get a job, and it will be a job in Surgery." She got up and leaned against the rain, a red-haired girl in a white dress that was soaked and flattened to her lithe figure. "Until then, I'll take what I can get."

But what of her professional pride, and what of Arch?

"He hasn't actually said he loved me," she reasoned, though her heart cried out in protest. "All he said was that my hair is a flame . . ."

She was looking into the choppy whitecaps atop the pattern of gray-green waves. It was deep here when the tide was in, doubly so when the northeast wind pushed the water shoreward from the Gulf outside the island over there. Wasn't that something down there?

Susan's mind rejected violently what her eyes saw. There was something moving just under the surface of the waves, a filmy something—a girl's silken robe.

The wet white shoes wanted to stick to Susan's stockings.

With a strength she didn't know her hands had, she yanked them off as she went into the water.

It was warmer than the rain. Her flesh knew this, but her consciousness was in her hands. They had hold of the flimsy fabric, then of the human body that was caught between the pilings of the pavilion.

Susan went down twice, using her body as an upward thrusting lever to pry the girl loose. She knew it was a girl. The fair hair that fanned responsively to the impetus of the waves told her.

Susan's lungs all but burst, her back refused to bear its burden, and then it did. She and that other girl were free to breathe. Susan did, in great gulps. She had to get the girl up on the dock.

It was impossible. There were barnacles on the pilings, and Susan's legs were cut and bleeding. Not wasting time in trying to climb onto the pier, Susan struck out for shore.

Surely someone would see them, help them; there might still be breath in this light body. There was the sound of gulls kreeing somewhere, and Susan felt the grayness darken as her strength waned.

Then strong hands found her, and lifted her.

CHAPTER V

The dome light, dimmed to candle volume, looked different from a hospital bed, Susan thought, opening her eyes.

Her feet were cold, and her hair was a damp lump under her neck. She sneezed, and Amy Stapleton, looking very professional in her starched organdie cap, came immediately to the bedside.

"How do you feel, Susan?" Amy wore a long face.

"Cold." Susan thought, *Why is Amy mad at me?* In her direct way, she asked, "Are you put out with me about something?" Then memory brought back the girl in the water. "Oh, Amy, was I too late?"

"Drink this, dear." Amy rolled up the head of the bed and poured a cup of tea, hot enough to be steaming.

The young nurse made no effort to stop the flow of Susan's tears. She offered a box of tissues; Susan took a handful and blew her noise vigorously. The door opened and Arch came in.

"Oh, Arch!" Tears welled up into Susan's eyes again, but this time she held them in check. How must she look, with her hair a wet, stringy mess and her nose red? She'd never be able to compete with the girl in the pink pinafore.

"Straighten up, girls. Himself is coming," Arch said seriously, but there was a twinkle in his brown eyes. "Himself" was the title bestowed by all the staff on the Administrator of St. Patrick's. Al—short for Aloysius—Duffy had been in charge of the hospital ever since it had moved from the ancient wooden building on the edge of town. That was twenty-five years ago. St. Patrick's then had been only "half an E," Susan always said. The new wing had come as a result of the impact of World War II on Palm City. There was a Navy installation nearby, now a permanent factor in the city's economy. Al Duffy had grown with the hospital.

He came in close on Arch's heels, his portly stomach preceding him.

"Well, Miss Farley, are you well enough to talk?" The

Administrator's eyes were still that startling blue that Susan remembered from her childhood visits to St. Patrick's for tonsillectomy and adenoid attention. The shock of thick hair that had been red, and was now snow-white, made the full face with its double chin seem more florid than it was. Al Duffy's best feature, though, was the large mouth, whose corners turned upwards in a kind of perpetual half-smile. *But he can look as cold as a Tibetan peak when he's stern,* Susan thought.

"Yes, sir." She swallowed in mid-word.

"What were you doing on the pavilion in the rain?" Himself asked.

"I was just starting back when I saw her robe in the water—" Susan shuddered uncontrollably.

Arch went over to the closet and took down a blanket from the shelf. Wordlessly, he placed it over Susan's feet. Her eyes thanked him, and she went on with her account.

"It was fortunate that your afternoon stroll took you to that particular spot," the older man said drily. "Do you often choose a rainstorm to go walking on the pier?"

"No, sir."

"Was there any particular reason why you did today?" The cold look was in the intensely blue eyes.

"A kind of personal reason, sir." Susan lifted her chin, and her own eyes were cool and unafraid. The worst had happened to her, and she wasn't going to let Al Duffy or anybody else bully her now. At least she could speak her mind without them firing her, because she didn't have a job at St. Patrick's, anyway. So she said, with no color at all in her clear voice, "I was saying goodbye to St. Patrick. We all kind of personalize the statue, sir. And after I'd walked that far, the pier seemed to beckon. There were gulls on the railing—" Her mind was turned toward the memory of the sodden pier planks and the wise, beady look of the birds. Wouldn't the girl's fall have made them fly? And she was sure they hadn't.

"You are leaving us?" The deep voice with the Irish roll in it had the right amount of surprise and regret, Susan thought. As if he didn't know. "It was my understanding you were going to be on our staff." He turned to Arch, who was at the foot of Susan's bed, his strong hands resting on the bedstead.

"She's going to work for Dr. Mitchell," Arch said, his brown eyes on Susan's.

So Arch didn't know. Susan felt a surge of relief. The

knowledge that he had known and didn't tell her about the closing of the ranks in the Nursing Services office had hurt as badly as the look of open admiration on his face for the girl in pink.

"No, sir, I'm not." Susan heard her voice speaking again. "I wanted so badly to work in Surgery that I changed my mind. And then Mrs. Branch told me there wasn't room for me there. So I went for a walk, to decide what I should do—leave Palm City or try for something else here. I didn't get around to making a decision, though. And now—now it doesn't seem to matter so much." Susan turned her head away from them all. She was seeing that fanning blonde hair, moving with the waves. Would she ever be able to wipe it out of her memory? She shivered again.

"The reporters are waiting on the sun porch, sir," Arch said respectfully. "Do you think Miss Farley is up to seeing them?"

Was there an implication in his deep voice that it wouldn't be wise for the press to know that a graduate nurse from St. Patrick's own nursing school had been refused a position, and was, in fact, trying to decide where to offer her services when she'd pulled a patient from the pilings underneath St. Patrick's private pier?

The Administrator looked at the young resident doctor from under his bushy gray brows. The very blue eyes were thoughtful. Whatever Arch had meant, Al Duffy was nobody's fool. He pursed his lips. "You're the doctor. What do you think?"

"I think she needs rest—she's been badly overworked lately, and worried about her father's condition. And as much as anything, I think she needs for her mind to be put at ease." Susan sneezed, and Arch came around to pick up her wrist and hunt for her pulse. "A thing like this could lead to pneumonia."

"I hope not." The huge body moved restlessly. "We can do this, however. We can relieve Miss Farley of the necessity of making a decision about leaving Palm City. It's impossible to put her in Surgery here, since Mrs. Branch has no vacancy at present, but St. Patrick's is badly in need of good nurses—in orthopedics, for instance." The Administrator walked over to the window. It was dark outside, but the lighted statue of St. Patrick was leaning against its serpent-wrapped staff. Susan held her breath. She saw that Amy was round-eyed. Everybody in the sprawling building would know that Himself had overridden Dr. Mitchell and

Ma Maggie. "Would you consider helping us in Second, East?" The Irish voice was firm. Himself knew what he was doing, but he didn't falter.

Susan drew a shaken breath.

"I'll be happy to, sir," she said.

The big man with the surprisingly light step walked to the door, and stopped to say a last word. "St. Patrick will be pleased," he said. The blue eyes twinkled. Then the white head disappeared.

Arch whistled softly, and Amy's sigh was an echo of Susan's.

"Let me get rid of the gentlemen of the press," Arch said. "I'll be right back. Don't you go for a walk." His long stride took him out.

"Amy, how's Dad?"

"Why don't you ask him?" Amy picked up the telephone and asked the operator to connect her with Room 418. She grinned, and handed the phone to Susan.

Grace's voice answered.

"Hi, honey." Susan was relieved to know that Grace was there. She didn't want her father to know that she was a fellow-patient. "Will you tell Dad that I'm doing some special duty and can't be there tonight? And I won't be home, dear. You might want to ask someone in."

"I know," Grace said with meaning. "I didn't expect you. Arch phoned me to come over. Dad is fine."

"Then maybe you can drop in here a little later?" Susan felt the fullness in the back of her throat again—everyone was good. Even Grace must be growing up. Her eyelids closed with sheer fatigue. From a vast distance she heard Arch when he came back in, felt the strength of his fingers when he picked up her wrist, heard him tell Amy she could go for supper. And then Susan slept.

But it was fitful sleep. She felt again the contrast of the warmth of the bay waters and the steely cold of the rain. Her legs stung with the salt water where the barnacles had made their lacerations. Her lungs were pain-shot from immersion. And there was that other girl— She awoke with a cry.

"It's all right, sweetheart." Arch was there; the light was on. How like him, knowing that she would not want to waken in the dark. And did she dream his calling her sweetheart?

"I had a bad dream," she said.

"I know." His fingers were strong, around hers. He

loosened them long enough to pull the string of her call light. An aide came.

"We'll have that tray, now, please," Arch said.

The tray materialized. Its covered silver dishes, opened, disclosed cream of chicken soup, salted crackers, a glass of milk, and half a peach.

"Eat up, girl, and then we'll give you a sleeping pill . . ."

"No." Susan sat up in bed. Her hair, almost dry now, fell in soft waves around her shoulders, covered by the plain hospital shirt. "I'm going to cut it," she muttered.

"Please don't," Arch said quietly.

She lifted a hand to coil it out of her way. How could she tell him about the other girl's hair, a silken web in the moving water? And then she did tell him. The last words were spoken against the starched white of his jacket, her tears dampening its immaculate front.

"Listen, Susan. Listen, sweet." Arch put his big hand against the back of her head and held her to him.

The pressure steadied Susan's heart. Gradually she stopped sobbing. "I think that'll be all," she said, using Amy's tissues.

"That's my girl. I believe you'll be better if you have the whole story now. I should have known you wouldn't seek refuge behind a sleeping pill." He eased her back against the pillows, and pushed the soup toward her. "Eat it and I'll tell you."

Susan obeyed. To her surprise, she discovered that she was hungry.

"The girl's name was Pamela Durrance. She came to St. Patrick's a week ago, to have a baby."

Susan gave a startled exclamation.

"She was vouched for by Dr. Howell."

Susan nodded. Dr. Howell was a specialist in obstetrics, and had one of the community's largest practices. Arch's deep voice went on.

"But Dr. Howell says he had seen her only once before, that she was a newcomer in Palm City. He said she hadn't had medical examination prior to her visit to him. Or so she said." Arch got up and began pacing back and forth in the limited space of the hospital room. He continued.

"The baby was born—a fine boy. I helped Dr. Howell on that one. There were no complications. She could have taken the baby home two days ago, but she asked to stay the extra time, 'until someone could get to Palm City to help take care of the baby,' she told the floor nurse." Arch rubbed his hand over his black hair in distress, a gesture that always made Susan want to smooth the black locks into place afterwards.

"She paid her bill when it was sent up this morning. She was to go home this evening. Of course she was ambulatory—she could have walked out onto the pier, and in good weather there would have been nothing extraordinary about it. She was strong, young, healthy—"

"Have her people been notified?" Susan asked, her eyes big with sympathy for this unknown girl.

"Himself called the name and the number on the card. No such person at the number given. He'd moved away. Somebody she put down as William Durrance. In St. Paul."

"What about the baby?" Susan's voice was small. This was real trouble.

"Yeah. What about the baby?" Arch stood and looked out at the lighted statue.

Susan opened her mouth to comment on the gulls. If Pamela Durrance had fallen in and flailed around in the water at the end of the pier, the gulls would have flown, wouldn't they? And they hadn't. They had sat in a row, lined up on the rail, facing into the wind, the rain dripping off their beaks.

"You hush, Susan Farley," she told herself. What good could it possibly do, now? And someday, perhaps that baby upstairs would be tall and proud and unshadowed by a young mother's death that, if Susan kept quiet, need not be labeled a suicide.

"Arch, I'm tired. I'd like to go to sleep, I think. And tell Amy she needn't stay—I'm fine. Be good as new in the morning."

The strange part of it was, Susan slept. Dreamlessly.

CHAPTER VI

It was difficult for Susan to adjust herself to the atmosphere of the eastern wing of the second floor, devoted exclusively to orthopedics.

In the first place, the patients here were sure to be in the hospital for long terms. A nurse got to know them, to like them or dislike them. In Surgery, Susan had been able to maintain an impersonal attitude, because surgery was decisive. It worked, or it didn't.

The Supervisor on Second, East, was an older woman. Susan was withholding an opinion of Mrs. Freeman. Her introduction as a part of the working force in orthopedics under Mrs. Freeman hadn't been auspicious.

She was early that first Monday morning, in order to make herself available for any indoctrination the Floor Supervisor might wish to give her. She knew Mrs. Freeman from her student stint on Second, East, but the students were a group then, herded about as such. This time, Susan was on her own. She wore her nicest uniform, the one that buttoned down the side front, a poplin outfit that snugged around Susan's slim waist and rounded hips, but gave ample walking room with its softly flared skirt. The dainty white organdie cap that denoted her graduation from St. Patrick's own school was perched on Susan's well-shaped head. The soft waves and heavy chignon of her dark-red hair were an attractive foil for the stark white of her clothes. Only the shoes were worn, though the freshly applied polish did its best to hide their long term of service.

None of this seemed to impress Mrs. Freeman. Her iron-gray head was bent over the charts when Susan reported for duty at ten minutes of seven. To Susan's greeting, she got a formal "good morning" in reply. No amplification.

Susan went around the end of the desk, and stood at the window looking down on the traffic that came and went along the curved driveway of the main entrance. Young nurses were being let out of all types and models of cars. They looked scrubbed and polished, the early morning sunlight glinting through the moss-hung live-oak trees on shining curls or simple hair-dos. Mostly they were kissed goodbye by husbands behind the wheel, the degree of fervor a matter of interest and amusement to the watching Susan. Her face sobered, however, at the sight of the older nurses and aides, coming often afoot down the half-moon pavement, walking with obvious effort on feet that had grown more and more painful from traversing miles of hospital corridors through the years. From this second-floor vantage point, Susan realized she was looking at a vignette of the private lives of St. Patrick's nurses, reporting for the seven-to-three shift, often considered the most arduous of the day.

Mrs. Freeman spoke from behind her, and Susan turned from her contemplation of the driveway. "Nice bit of newspaper prominence you gave the hospital," the Supervisor said.

Susan raised her dark eyebrows in surprise. Did Mrs. Freeman mean to imply that she was a publicity seeker? Quickly she drew her lids down, her heart-shaped face seeming to withdraw behind a curtain. "Yes, Mrs. Freeman," she managed to say. She'd give her superior the benefit of the doubt. Time would tell whether the comment was malicious or not. And if so, what? Nothing, Susan answered herself. She was going to be a fixture in St. Patrick's, Mrs. Freeman or no Mrs. Freeman.

But the morning was interminable. Susan threw herself into the routine of orthopedics with everything she had; she carried trays, fed one patient whose right arm was in traction, helped aides make beds, gave bedpans, undertook to give a bath to a woman in a cast from her hips to her neck who refused to allow any of the others to do so, saying that she'd been maltreated by everyone on the floor; she was giving a post-operative intravenous when Mrs. Freeman came to the door and asked her to report to the desk when she was through.

Susan was too tired to smile a reply, but she murmured, "Yes, Mrs. Freeman." She passionately wanted the staff on this floor to like her.

"Two-twelve is a compound, comminuted fracture of the left humerus," Mrs. Freeman told her when she stopped at the desk. "Here's the chart. Sit down over there and digest it thoroughly."

Susan pulled a stool from under the shelf at the window and sat with her back to the desk and the long corridor that reached the length of this eastern wing of St. Patrick's. The patient in Room 212 was a white male, Oliver Cox by name, age forty-one; he had broken his elbow in a fall backward, the break a long one, with a protrusion of the bone through the flesh in the upper arm; a small triangle of the bone was broken clear. It was assumed that the bone had made contact with the ground. The patient was allergic to tetanus antitoxin. There had been a conference of four doctors, whose signatures were on the chart. All agreed on the desirability of mobility in the joint, and a cast was ruled out by all. A traction had been established. Hospitalization for a minimum of three weeks was indicated. A private duty nurse was requested by the patient.

At this point, Susan looked up. Mrs. Freeman was posting charts after the visits of doctors on their morning rounds. "Does he have a special?" she asked.

Mrs. Freeman didn't reply. Susan caught her full lower lip between her teeth, and subdued her impulse to speak what she thought, the trait that had caused her so much difficulty all her life.

When she finished with the chart, she quietly hung it on the hook over which a cellophane-covered number denoted the room of the patient. She waited, this time, until Mrs. Freeman was not engaged. It seemed quite a while.

"The register has no nurses available for two-twelve." Mrs. Freeman spoke each word with clipped precision. She wasted nothing on expression. Susan decided that her face was chiseled out of marble. "The patient is a close friend of Dr. Mitchell's. We wish him to be comfortable, as much so as we can make him," she went on.

"Certainly," Susan said into the pause Mrs. Freeman left. What did the old termagant suppose, that Susan would ignore the needs of Dr. Mitchell's friend? Susan felt her back stiffen.

"When you are on duty, you will, whenever possible, take over the care of two-twelve." The Supervisor turned back to her work.

Ignoring her fatigue, Susan walked briskly down the hall to Room 212. The door was open, in defiance of the air-conditioning, and the curtains billowed in from the open window. The Venetian blind was up; the room was filled with the brightness of the noon world outside. There was a broad view of the bay, and the summer flowers in the beds that lined the walks wafted their fragrance through the double windows. Every inch of space in the room was taken up with floral arrangements. Several were on the floor. The patient was awake.

"Hi, beautiful," Oliver Cox greeted Susan. "Are you my special nurse?" He seemed pleased at the prospect.

Susan sighed inwardly. He was going to be one of those male patients who thought it necessary to be exaggeratedly flippant with the nurses. She had encountered this often during her student days, and had decided that it was because men couldn't bear for young women to consider their illnesses a mark of unmanliness.

"No, sir, I'm regularly on duty on this floor," she replied.

He looked at her name in its neat frame, pinned to her uniform. "Miss Farley, the first thing I'd like you to do for me is to get rid of some of these funeral wreaths." He waved his free hand toward the flowers. "Can't you give 'em to some of the other patients?"

"I'll be glad to." Susan bent to pick up the nearest container on the floor. She thought how much her father would have enjoyed this potted plant, a profusely blooming yellow chrysanthemum. But he had gone home yesterday. Anyway, that decision was for Mrs. Freeman to make. Dutifully, Susan took the plant to the desk.

"He wants some of these sent to other rooms," she explained.

"It's time for his Demerol," Mrs. Freeman said.

Susan prepared the hypodermic and put it on the sterile tray.

"What's that?" Oliver Cox demanded when she went back to his room.

"This is the pain medication," Susan answered primly.

"Take it away. It makes me feel fuzzy. I've got to think . . ."

Susan took it away. She reported to Mrs. Freeman that 212 wanted no sedation.

"I'll call the doctor; it was specifically ordered."

But the doctor, when reached, sustained Oliver Cox in his refusal. The patient rose a notch in Susan's regard. She wondered, walking the endless steps entailed by call lights and regular chores, what Oliver Cox had to think about that made him prefer pain to relief. He was becoming an individual to her, rather than the traction case in Room 212.

When his light went on next, Susan smiled at the small joke he made about wanting his feet raised. "I'm in a race," he said apologetically, as if he regretted causing trouble, "and I have to pick up my feet." He thanked her, and then as she turned to go, he spoke again.

"Farley. Farley. Oh, you're the one . . ." Susan felt her heart sink. She supposed this would go on until people forgot about Pamela Durrance.

"Yes, sir." From the hospital's point of view, it was a regrettable incident, and the least said the better. This had been strongly emphasized to Susan by Al Duffy himself.

"What's become of the baby?"

"He's in the nursery, here."

"What'll become of him?"

"I don't know." Susan again started to leave.

"Look, Miss Farley." Oliver Cox had salt-and-pepper hair that was cut shorter than anyone's Susan had ever seen. Heavy brows, still untouched by gray, grew low over black eyes that were set deep in a strong face. His cheeks were as lean as Arch's, but the cheekbones were higher, and the lips were thin enough to be almost nonexistent. The mouth was a straight line across the lower face, somehow emphasizing the strength of the long jaw below it. A man accustomed to power, and ruthless enough to use it.

Susan walked back to the bed.

"Mine is not an idle interest," he told her. "I'm no gossiper. I want to know what disposition is going to be made of that baby."

"I actually don't know," Susan told him sincerely. "But I will find out or send someone in who can answer you with authority."

She made a mental note to talk to Arch about this. They were going to have dinner together, at the Farley bungalow, since Susan wanted Grace to be free this evening after being with their father all afternoon. Mornings, the cleaning woman was "sitting" as well.

"If I weren't trussed up here like a chicken on a rotisserie," he growled, "I'd—" He clamped his mouth and the strong face scowled. "Never mind, Miss Farley. You run ahead. Don't bother to mention it further—I'll work it out."

Arch had an emergency at the hospital and couldn't come to dinner that night, after all. And Susan was so tired that, after getting her father ready for bed, she showered and got into bed herself. She opened her book for her self-imposed hour of study on cancer research, a daily duty no matter what.

Her fingers were almost too tired to make notes. "300,000 will develop cancer in the United States this year," she wrote. "There will be 200,000 deaths of this disease. Treatment improves and cure rates rise, but so does incidence. Losing battle. Cancer research, public and private, costing now more than seventy-five million a year." She paused, visualizing the army of men and women engaged in this war of test tubes and clinical experiments. She had attended every lecture the hospital had held about cancer, and as the experts came and went, she had wondered if perhaps the very immensity of the program—carried on by so many agencies, bureaus, hospitals, university laboratories, and public health services—didn't result in duplication of effort and even discoveries.

"Well, better brains than mine are living with this problem," she told herself as she turned out the light. But her thoughts kept her awake.

Her mother had fought until the very last breath to stay with her husband and daughters. Up from the depths of the dulling sedation, she had fought time and again, to plead that someone do something to help her to breathe. Susan looked wide-eyed into the darkness of her room, and prayed that her father would be spared a similar agony.

She was just dozing off when she remembered the stern look on Oliver Cox's face when he'd told her he would work out the problem of young Pat Durrance's life. Patrick was the name the hospital authorities had given the boy baby whom no one had come forward to claim.

"St. Patrick has a special interest in this one," Al Duffy had told Susan.

And now someone else seemed to have a special interest. *Two-twelve is just the one who can do something about it,* Susan thought sleepily. The man was a caged thing, lying there with his left arm suspended by a wire run through the bones and flesh of his wirst. It seemed to infuriate him because the crippled limb refused to make a fist. He worked his fingers in a constant effort to make it do so.

"He's quite a guy," Susan told herself. "He'll fight himself free of the hospital before any three weeks."

But when Susan reported for duty the following day, she found the man in Room 212 delirious. The infection that raged in his blood, born of the bone's contact with germ-ridden earth, had laid low the man's indomitable will to immediate recovery.

Amy Stapleton was on as his special. Susan didn't see him for days.

When she did, he sent for her.

CHAPTER VII

"I think he's some big union official from up North," Arch answered Susan's question about the identity of the man in Room 212.

They were having dinner on the beach, having picked up two fried-chicken box lunches from a drive-in on the causeway that did a land-office business.

To Susan's insistence that she bring the lunch, Arch had shaken his head firmly. "Nope. I've eaten at your house too many times now; it's my turn. A resident's salary doesn't run to the Chateau, but we can enjoy the same surf, watch the same moon rise."

They wore their bathing suits under beach wear. It was Susan's first outing all summer; her father's illness had cast a shadow between her and the sun. The evening with Arch began to assume the atmosphere of a full-fledged celebration. Susan even managed to banish the girl in the pink pinafore from her mind, although she had learned some time ago that the girl's name was Mavis Pennington. She operated the Hospitality Cart at the hospital on Tuesdays. And, a bit of knowledge that made Susan's heart sink even lower, the glamorous Mavis was Dr. Mitchell's niece. *Everywhere I turn, that man's ahead of me*, Susan had thought miserably.

Since that night when she herself had been a patient, Arch hadn't called her sweetheart again. He'd been his old friendly, understanding self, but the electricity that had been in the atmosphere that night in the elevator, and later when she was as wet as a half-drowned rat, had been missing. Susan had to admit, however, that she hadn't been alone with him. Both of them had been too busy.

This was the first opportunity she'd had to talk with him about the forceful patient in Room 212.

They were driving down the mile-long ribbon of hard sand beach on Gull Island. It was low tide now, and Arch thought they'd better have their swim on the incoming tide, then enjoy their picnic supper. He had Cokes in crushed ice in a bucket in the trunk.

"He's been here in Palm City ever since Christmas," Susan

remarked, Oliver Cox still nagging at her mind. He was better; she'd been in to see him during the day, and she thought he'd been glad to see her. "Though I don't understand why. Amy is twice as good as I am on private duty, and she's pretty enough to hang on the wall."

"She is, indeed. But Amy–forgive my criticizing your friend, I'm not, really, just analyzing–Amy bustles." Arch laughed, remembering Amy's cheerful housekeeping in the sickroom.

"All Amy's patients say she's the neatest thing in the world," Susan defended her.

"That's just what I mean. I was in to see Cox twice during this week, and I give you my word, Amy fluffed the pillows, straightened the spread, rattled newspapers putting them in the wastebasket, got fresh water both times, and dusted the glass top of the dresser for good measure." Arch looked speculatively at the sand on his right, appraising it for parking purposes. He had to put the car where the incoming tide wouldn't reach it, but he didn't want to be unable to pull out. It would be tricky business, getting stuck in the powdery sand after dark.

"He said his work was electrical contracting." Susan went back to Cox.

"It is. He saw to the electrical work of a subdivision on the west end of town that Doc Mitchell is financing. That's how they got to know each other. His men like him a lot, I understand."

"How could you ever know that?" Susan was teasing.

"I've treated some of them in Emergency. Cuts, a broken finger or two–they all take time to run upstairs to look in on Cox."

"I wondered about the steady parade of men in work helmets and any old kind of clothes. They pay not the slightest attention to visiting hours. One came in last night at midnight, the night duty nurse told me." Susan's voice conveyed her opinion of such disregard of hospital rules.

"Oh?" Arch was only mildly interested. Cox was recuperating, and what he did was his personal physician's business, not the resident's. Susan accepted his reply to mean that Cox as a topic of conversation wasn't too rewarding. She had meant to ask him about the man's interest in the Durrance baby. A day never passed that Oliver Cox didn't inquire about what was, in his language, "the hospital's baby."

Arch put the emergency brake on, and got out, coming around to open the door for Susan. She took the hand he offered, and stepped onto the warmth of the sand, still reflecting its stored heat of the afternoon. She slipped off her sandals immediately, finding the feel of the beach delightful to hospital-tired feet.

The sunset was startlingly beautiful. Vivid peach and lemon yellow shading to deep ochre reached from one end of the western horizon to the other. The far end of the island was a curved hook into the sea, one of the rare spots on the Gulf Coast crescent that was being built up by the deposit of sand rather than eroded by tides and storms. Tonight, Susan thought, there must be a beached fish or something out on the little cape, for hundreds of water birds were flying low, landing, hopping around, being startled, and taking off again. Silhouetted against the color-flags of the sky behind them, the sight was primitive and stirring.

Arch opened the trunk and hunted for beach towels, while Susan folded her discarded play skirt and hung it over the car door. She was wearing Grace's bathing suit, a bright blue elasticized satin that did things for her red hair and blue eyes. Her own suit was pink. Susan had looked at it with disfavor, thinking that she wouldn't go swimming again until she could afford a new one. To her surprise, Grace had offered hers. *I guess a distaste for some particular outfit is one of the things Grace understands,* Susan thought. *I'm grateful, anyway, for whatever reason.*

She had cause to be. The blue suit went well with the sea and the sand and the sunset. She was suddenly and unaccountably happy.

"I'll race you in," she called to Arch, and ran on feet that seemed winged into the breakers.

Arch was close behind her. Both of them dived cleanly into the furling roll of a ground swell, their heels cutting the froth just as the wave broke. Swimming well was a prerequisite for a Florida girl's upbringing. And Susan had seen to it that Grace, too, was at home in the water. Nothing, she thought, her uncapped head breaking the surface, was as exhilarating as this. She raced the next roller inshore. It dragged at her feet when she reached for bottom, and she had to exert a bit of effort to free herself of the undertow. Arch was floating, out beyond the line of breakers.

She knew a sudden, sharp loneliness. That other girl, the one with the long, fair hair—couldn't she swim? Susan shook her head vigorously, the salt water flying from her face and hair. Her pleasure in the water was gone. "I'm going in," she called to Arch. He waved at her, not hearing, but understanding.

Toweling her hair, Susan watched Arch turn over and begin to swim lazily toward shore. *I'm glad we have this end of the beach to ourselves*, she thought, slipping her arms into her terry-cloth robe. *That's one of the wonderful things about this section of Florida's coast. Solitude like this, the unalloyed enjoyment of a sunset free of smoke haze, would never be possible downstate, either on the east coast or the west.*

She went about the task of spreading a cloth that she'd brought for the lunches. Arch Curtis needn't think she wasn't going to bring along a few trimmings for their picnic. She smiled to herself, putting out paper plates, anchoring paper napkins with a silver fork for each place. Then she began to hum, savoring to the full the isolation of pine-grown dunes behind them, the cape to the west, with the lighthouse just beginning to show its revolving eye, and the limitless expanse of restless Gulf.

She waved a towel to Arch, a signal to come to supper. *Downright domestic, this is*, she thought contentedly. Maybe this was the night for the electricity to come back.

And then her brows met in a quick frown. Why didn't Arch come on? He was going around in splashing circles, a bit east of where she'd seen him last.

The last level rays of the setting sun reflected against a silver triangle in the center of the circle Arch was making in his great strokes for freedom.

Susan's heart froze in her breast. She never remembered taking off the terry-cloth robe, or running on flying feet into the surf. But she knew that she would remember to her dying day the sight of the great tiger shark as it turned on its side to shorten the circumference of Arch's frenzied circling.

Susan didn't have any idea of what she was going to do. Arch Curtis was one of the finest athletes she knew. He was a superb swimmer. And he knew about sharks.

But he was in trouble. And whether she could help or not, Susan was going to him.

Oh, God, make me able to help! Her silent prayer was her only thought as she used her fast crawl stroke.

There is little twilight in the tropics, but in summer, the day lingers, regretful to pull down the curtain of night. Because it was midsummer, Arch Curtis survived his battle with the tiger shark.

He had stopped flailing around when Susan got within calling distance. On shore, he explained that he'd gotten a cramp.

"A lousy, stupid leg cramp. Not even a belly cramp. Just a knot in the calf of my leg as big as my hat, and I knew I was done for. And when you had me by the hair. Wow!" He rubbed his sore scalp gently.

"If you'd had the kind of haircut Oliver Cox has, I'd have missed you," she said, wrapping the big beach towel around Arch's shuddering shoulders. "I could just barely get hold—and what else could I grasp? There should be a law about men's bathing suits; trunks aren't for the swimmer with a cramp."

Neither of them spoke of the shark just then. Horror lived in the unforgettable picture of those needlelike teeth, those snapping jaws.

Arch was fine, he said insistently. But his lips were blue, and Susan insisted that she wasn't hungry, anyway.

"Hot coffee for us," she told him. "At my house."

They were quiet during the long drive across the causeway and through the neon-lighted streets of Palm City. When they got to the Farley bungalow, Arch was having a chill.

Susan shoved him ahead of her up the porch steps.

"A hot bath's the thing," she insisted.

Obediently, Arch got into her father's flannel robe while the steaming water filled the old-fashioned tub. Then she told Grace about the shark.

Grace was putting fresh lacquer on her nails; she waved them in an effort to dry them more quickly, her great brown eyes sparkling with excitement. John Farley was asleep in the big back bedroom that had been his and his wife's for thirty-two years.

Susan hurriedly changed into fresh clothes.

She was beating eggs preparatory to scrambling them when she realized that, in her distraught condition, she had put on a cotton dress that was undoubtedly starched and fresh and becoming, with its full skirt and scoop neck, but also undeniably pink. She stood in the middle of the big kitchen and made a chopping gesture of anger with the hand that held the egg-beater. Golden drops of egg fell onto the clean linoleum.

"Look what you're doing!" Grace was horrified. It had been her day to clean the floor, since the cleaning woman had done the nursing stint today. "What in the world is the matter with you?" Still fussing, she wiped up the vagrant egg with a damp sponge. "This is a crazy kind of picnic—scrambled eggs. What's the matter with the chicken? Can I get the boxes out of the car? I'm hungry, too, Susan . . . What did you say?" Grace thought she must have been mistaken. She would have sworn that Susan said something about her dress.

Susan pressed her lips together. In her hurry to get some hot food ready for Arch when he was ready for it, she had chosen the one dress she shouldn't have. Unfortunately there was no time to change it.

When Arch came in, wearing John Farley's too-short trousers and a T-shirt of his own from the car, he whistled at the picture Susan made, buttering toast at the breakfast table. However, he said the wrong thing.

"Honey, you're a picture a man dreams of. That sure is one pretty pink whatchamacallit you have on."

The whatchamacallit was a pink-and-white-checked pinafore.

Susan was out of sorts all evening.

Arch, bewildered, went home early.

CHAPTER VIII

"I believe Himself knows something about our baby," Amy told Susan when they met in the kitchen of Second, East, for coffee the next day.

"Really?" Susan felt a quickening of her pulse. Pat Durrance was growing visibly from day to day. His hair was nonexistent, but his infinitesimal eyebrows were now the same golden fairness of his mother's. "He's getting to be a person," Susan said. "Isn't it a bit early for him to grin like that?" She considered Amy an authority; in Amy's family there were steps of children descending downward in years from Amy's twenty to six.

"No," Amy replied practically, emptying the coffee grounds from the basket of the new percolator contributed to the floor kitchen by her patient. Oliver Cox liked his coffee whenever he awakened, which was invariably around four o'clock in the morning. The battered aluminum kettle on the old hot plate took longer to make coffee than he cared to wait. After the first day, a deliveryman had brought a case of vacuum-packed coffee, the new twelve-cup percolator, and an attractive breakfast set of Japanese china. Mr. Cox also liked to drink out of a thin cup.

"What makes you think Mr. Duffy has found out about Pamela Durrance?" Susan took a swallow of coffee that nearly scorched her tongue.

"He's been spending a lot of time with Mr. Cox. They ask me to leave the room while they talk. And they talk, talk. You don't eavesdrop on Himself—if he seeks privacy, to be polite a person has to retreat to the next floor." Amy grinned, remembering the rolling r's that came from behind the closed door of Room 212. "I went all the way to the far end of the sun parlor to keep from hearing, but when Himself says 'Patrrrick,' the angels aren't the only ones who listen."

"Arch told me that Oliver Cox is an electrical union official from somewhere up North," Susan commented. She wasn't going to quiz Amy about her patient's background, but if *she* volunteered information and Amy followed suit, she comforted herself that there was no violation of ethics.

"He thinks that all these new plants opening up in the South should be organized," Amy said importantly, "but he came down here to see that it was done according to Hoyle, and not by any of these strong-arm tactics that have gotten the labor movement into such disrepute in the big industrial areas." She almost gave out of breath, making her memorized contribution.

"Why, Amy! Listen to who's an expert labor-relations theorist!" All this was interesting to Susan, and she knew it would be to her father, whose major had been political economy.

"I think he knew Pat's mother." Amy put down her cup and turned to leave, having set off her conversational bombshell.

"*Amy!* Don't you dare leave now," Susan said.

Amy's laughter was stopped by the entrance of the Floor Supervisor. The nurses were permitted to have coffee in the floor kitchen, but Mrs. Freeman discouraged coffee *and* conversation.

"The call lights make Second, East, look like a Main Street decorated for Christmas, Miss Farley. But it isn't Christmas, it's July." She withdrew to her command post behind the desk.

Susan was sure she heard Amy mutter, "Brrrrr, I thought it was January."

Smothering her own impulse to giggle, she and Amy separated, Amy to go back to her charge, and Susan to answer the three lights. Orthopedics was sparsely populated this morning. Three patients had gone home, and wheeling them down to the ambulance entrance accounted for the absence of nurses' aides from the floor. Her sense of justice told her that Mrs. Freeman was within her rights to cut short their coffee break. They had been out of circulation a full ten minutes. Full of self-condemnation, Susan hurried to put things right.

Whether it was because she was moving more swiftly than usual, or because the pitcher was moist on the outside, but in taking a bedside ice-water pitcher for refilling, she dropped it on the terrazzo floor of the corridor. It made a resounding crash, and water and broken glass were scattered everywhere. She went immediately for something to clean it up. The janitor's closet was around the corner, so

Susan was out of sight when Dr. Mitchell came striding along, chin up and greeting patients through the open doorways.

Susan, mop and dustpan in hand, came around the corner just as Dr. Mitchell was abreast of Room 212. The Chief of Staff hadn't, apparently, intended to call on Oliver Cox, but changed his mind when Cox spoke to him from inside the open door. At any rate, the Chief turned on his heel, and in doing so, his feet slipped out from under him and he went down. Unfortunately, the shards of glass awaited him on the highly waxed floor.

Susan was horrified to see that the doctor's right hand was bleeding from an ugly cut between the thumb and the forefinger.

"Oh, sir—" She bent over to help him to his feet, and Amy came swiftly from Cox's room to take his other arm.

The Chief of Staff shook them off. "I can get up by myself, thanks," he said stiffly.

"It's all my fault," Susan said contritely. "I dropped the pitcher. I'd gone for these—" The mop and dustpan were on the floor where she'd put them to help the doctor.

"Remove those booby-traps, Miss Farley." Mrs. Freeman came up behind Susan on silent feet. "Call the janitor to clean up your mess. St. Patrick's nurses aren't charwomen. Not usually."

Susan's face flamed. She did Mrs. Freeman's bidding, leaving Dr. Mitchell to be escorted by the clucking Floor Supervisor to Surgery. From the public-address box on the wall came the monotone of the dispatcher:

"Dr. Curtis . . . Dr. Curtis . . ."

Susan thought hysterically, *Arch will sew the Chief up, but who will mend my shattered dignity?*

And then the implication of the right-hand cut on Dr. Mitchell's hand struck her. He wouldn't be able to operate for at least a week!

All day, as Susan went about her chores, the specter of what she had caused followed her. The only bright spot, surprisingly enough, was the visit she had with Oliver Cox.

Amy had met her in the hall and suggested that she look in on the saturnine patient in Room 212.

Susan found him sitting up in bed, his injured arm high in the air, the heavy weights that were suspended from the miniature pulley adjusting the limb so that Cox could move about. When Susan entered, he was eyeing the cast-iron pipe of the traction frame that made a sort of superstructure to his bed.

"The longshore boys are going to get onto you medical folks, infringing on their racket," he greeted her. "This gear looks like loading rigging on a freighter."

"I'll bet they are more sure-footed than you are," Susan said with mock-severity. "It's astonishing how many of you powerfully built men come in here with broken bones. How *could* you fall backwards?" Susan thought she was coaxing the patient to talk about himself, usually a good sickroom procedure.

She was surprised at the reaction of the man in the bed. His lean, dark face clouded at her question. He looked at her sharply from beneath the starkly black brows. And made what was apparently a direct change of subject.

"Are you married to the idea of working in this joint?"

"Well, not exactly," Susan said, willing to follow his conversational lead. "What I dream of doing is something constructive about cancer."

"Why?" The black eyes were piercingly intense.

"I believe cancer is man's greatest physical enemy."

"We're spending enough money to do something about it," Cox said. "You medical people must be asleep at the switch."

"It does seem so," Susan admitted. "The amount of actual money spent is enormous. When you add to that the man-hours the world loses, the thing defies a price tag. But I couldn't possibly view it so statistically. It's a human problem—a personal problem—to me."

"Yeah. If you're so sharp, why didn't you go into the research angle? I hear they're the boys who do the job." He frowned. "What are you doing here on a bone floor? Why aren't you in the lab?"

"I considered the laboratory," Susan answered slowly, "but it would have taken a lot more education than I could afford to get—and I had to be earning money as soon as possible. This seemed the best answer."

"You know something about where all the money goes?"

"There's so much of it—my own knowledge is very superficial," Susan replied.

"Sit down. Pull your chair over here a bit closer. This is something my boys ought to know about. We got a disability pension program that's costing us plenty for this cancer thing." The frown was one of concentration, Susan thought. "Not that we ain't sorry for 'em; don't get me wrong. But it'd be good business for all of us if we could do something about it. You keep on talking, if it won't get you in bad with old Mrs. Little America."

Susan smiled at the apt description of Mrs. Freeman.

"As a matter of fact," she said, "Mrs. Freeman instructed me to do anything I could to make your path smoother." But she got up and looked out into the hall to survey the call-light situation. There were none on, so she came back.

"You smooth, like the lady said." He smiled, showing beautiful white teeth. It lighted up the whole dark face, Susan thought. It was the first time she'd seen Oliver Cox smile. *I like him,* she thought with surprise.

"Of course you know that the effort is divided into two phases, treatment and research. My own study has been in the first phase, though a person picks up a smattering of the other if one reads far enough. You should really talk to Dr. Curtis about this. He directed *my* study," Susan said.

"I'm talking to you," Cox said with characteristic brusqueness.

He's an arrogant man, Susan thought, but she was pleased. After a moment, she went on.

"You know, I suppose, that a lot of work has been done to discover a simple blood test to show whether or not cancer is present in the body. Without much success, I'm sorry to say. There are, however, some special methods—microscopic examinations of some of the body fluids and chemical tests—to aid in the diagnosis of cancer of certain parts of the body. The wives of your men would be helped by periodic examinations. But of course you must have a medical educational program that tells them these things." Her cornflower-blue eyes regarded him seriously.

"Go on," he told her, without replying directly.

"It's awful to think that if each person had regular examinations, most of the cancer deaths wouldn't occur. The American Cancer Society and the United States Public Health Service, as well as the National Cancer Institute, spend some of that money 'your boys' contribute telling people all this. Young people and older people. Cancer, unfortunately, picks no special age group." She stopped, seeing a question in his expressive eyes.

"But are they *getting* anywhere?" Impatiently, he brushed aside all the barriers of ignorance and lethargy.

"Oh, yes. Fifteen years ago, one in four of the wives of

whom we spoke died; now that number has been halved. And cancer of the large intestine—"

"Yeah?" Cox sat up straighter. The weights on the traction lowered as his arm raised higher with his altered position. He grunted involuntarily as his arm twinged with pain. But his attention remained riveted on Susan.

There was a sharp knock on the ground-glass upper half of the door, and it was shoved sharply inward. Mrs. Freeman's expressionless face appeared.

"Miss Farley, may I have a little of your time?" she asked with acidulous sweetness.

"Yes, ma'am." Susan got up hastily. She had no business to be caught sitting talking to a patient. Even this patient, privileged though he was. A nurse was permitted to talk, standing, to convey that the conversation was temporary, and that other duties existed. Susan had learned her professional-demeanor lessons, but she wasn't applying them. She was thinking, *Oh, Lord! Maybe I'm just not cut out to be a hospital nurse.* How could she get so wrapped up in her favorite subject as to let—what had Mr. Cox called Mrs. Freeman?—Mrs. Little America catch her off base?

But she reckoned without Oliver Cox. His reaction was immediate and characteristic.

"Hey, Mrs. Freeman!"

The Supervisor came back, polite but impatient.

"I want to see Dr. Mitchell as soon as it's convenient. I've been asking Miss Farley some questions that make me think perhaps the doc could do me some good."

"Yes, Mr. Cox." Mrs. Freeman smiled frostily. The look she gave Susan, standing still because the older woman was blocking the door, was, however, unforgiving.

"One more thing, Miss Farley," Cox said in the tone that always brought obedience from people. Susan waited, her hand on the doorknob.

"You've given me an idea. Will you come back when you're off duty? I'd like to talk to you about it. Bring Curtis along. You two might be a big help to my boys." His good hand waved her along.

Susan went, conscious of the disapproval of Mrs. Freeman, but inwardly aglow with anticipation over her visit with Oliver Cox after hours.

When she had an opportunity, she went looking for Arch.

He wasn't in Surgery; the nurse in the Recovery Room said he'd gone downstairs to the cafeteria for coffee. Susan looked at the big wall clock. If she hurried, she could spare enough time to ask him to meet her in Room 212 after the three o'clock change of shifts.

Arch usually sat at the table to the far right, where they had sat that night after her father's operation. Susan's seeking eyes found him there now.

He wasn't alone, however. Sitting opposite him, and laughing, her head with its cap of dark curls thrown back to show a soft chin and graceful throat line, was the pretty niece of Dr. Mitchell. Arch, laughing at the joke they shared, waved at Susan.

Susan waved back, and went on through the big room, making her way out the far door as if her errand took her that way. She wouldn't for the world have turned around and gone out, nor would she have intruded.

She was, she thought, always on the verge of tears these days. She wasn't going to cry now, though. Arch wasn't going to come from Mavis Pennington's delightful laughter to find Susan with a red nose and inflamed eyes.

She left her message with the dispatcher. It gave her a grim sort of pleasure to hear the monotonous summons come from the call box when she got back to Second, East.

"Dr. Curtis . . . Dr. Curtis," the voice said with mechanical unemphasis.

"That'll fix Miss Pink Pinafore," Susan said to herself.

She took special pains to repair the ravages of the past few hours before going to Oliver Cox's room at three.

CHAPTER IX

Oliver Cox looked anything but well when Susan came in. His face was gray with pain.

"That blasted X-ray hoodlum needled me into turning on my left side, and this punctured wing made a barrel roll," he told her.

Susan asked if he wouldn't like to have a hypodermic, and he scowled at her from beneath his bushy black brows.

"How can I talk sense to you and the doc if I'm all fuzzed up with old-lady medicine?" He did, however, consent to swallow two aspirin tablets.

Ordinarily Susan would have gone to the desk to request that the medication for Room 212 be secured from the pharmacy. But now, she pulled on the call light. "I'm a disgrace at the desk," she said mournfully. "Even though Mrs. Freeman is off duty, she leaves behind her the climate of disapproval."

Arch came in as Oliver Cox put down the water glass.

"Sit down, you two," Cox told them. "I want to ask you some questions." With his one good hand he fumbled around in the bedside table drawer and drew out a pencil and scratch pad. He thrust them toward Susan. "Put down what I say," he growled.

"What's this?" Arch asked.

Susan didn't answer him. This was Cox's party. She bent over the pad, the soft waves of her red hair glinting in the sunlight that filtered through the Venetian blind. Arch threw her a puzzled look.

"Your girl has been telling me about cancer—" Cox began.

"Oh?" Arch put one ankle over the other knee, and stretched his long frame so that he was sitting almost on the back of his neck. Man-fashion, he was in the one comfortable chair in the room. Susan sat primly in the straight chair, knees together, note pad on her lap. She was there, but she wasn't participating in this until she knew what the score was. She kept her lids over her blue eyes; Arch's nearness had started the familiar static disturbance that resulted in what Susan thought of as "an accelerated pulse and shallow respiration."

"A man laying in bed like this, strung up on a wire he could pull in two with his bare hands if he was man enough," Cox said, "does a lot of thinking. Maybe if I hadn't had that fight and been knocked off my pins, I never would'a got this idea I'm going to tell you about." He stopped and drew a deep breath.

For the first time since the young doctor had come into the room, Susan and Arch looked at each other. Susan's eyes telegraphed her awareness of Cox's mention of a fight, and Arch's expression said he noticed it, too. Cox's record stated he had stepped backward off a porch.

The shrewd eyes of the man against the pillows never missed a thing. "Yeah, I was clobbered. Trying to talk some sense into a hotheaded fool who had everything to live for. Fellow named Durrance."

The consonants and vowels that, combined, made a name which had brought a barrage of publicity to St. Patrick's and Susan echoed against the impersonal walls of Room 212. Susan drew a sharp breath. Arch showed his professional training by not reacting at all.

"Bill Durrance worked for me," Cox went on. "He and his wife were nothing but kids. She was going to have a baby. He was spending his spare time in Millville, drunk and gambling away every cent he made. I always figured what a man did in his off time was his own business, long as he did his job, but in this case," the sharp black eyes looked into space, heavy with memory, "I couldn't see what was going on without putting in my oar. Maybe if I'd kept my big mouth shut, things would have worked out. But I didn't . . ." There was quiet for a moment, the sound of waves against the seawall sending up their reminder that the bay had been the undoing of Pamela Durrance. The big double windows of Cox's room were kept open because of that sleep-inducing sound.

"Anyway, I was flat on my back when it happened. Bill was playing the numbers. He claimed he'd won, and went to collect from the shyster who sold him the strip of sixes. He was drunk, of course, from premature celebrating. The fellow contested Bill's claim, and Bill went for him like he did for me. Only the other guy had a gun, and in the scuffle it went off. Witnesses—barflies and bums—claim Bill hit the first lick, and that he had gotten hold of the gun when it went off. So there was no question of the law. Bill's wife," Cox paused at this point, "she'd just come down here to be with Bill when the baby came. They got no folks." There was another one of those pauses, filled with meaning.

Susan was seeing the fanning hair under the moving water. Arch got up and began pacing back and forth.

"Now the baby's got none, either." Cox took another breath, his face impassive. Then he went on.

"I'm not a family man, myself," he said. "Unless you could say my boys are my family." This time, there was the hint of a smile on the thin lips.

"And that brings us to what I want to talk about. Miss Farley was telling me about how folks with cancer could maybe be cured. Maybe never get that far. I got a boy working for me in Washington who's had some surgery for cancer—they cut his abdomen from here to here." The restless right hand described a half circle across Cox's own middle. "He's not well yet. What were the figures the old lady stopped you from telling me?" The sharp eyes fixed themselves on Susan.

She thought she'd never seen a man with such burning directness in his look. And she was beginning to think that Oliver Cox had more personal loyalty to his friends than any ten average men. It was a heart-warming trait. She looked to Arch before answering.

Arch stopped his pacing. Hands in pockets, he lifted his shoulders, indicating that she was to answer rather than he.

"Thirty per cent of intestinal cancer patients get well after five years of treatment," Susan said obediently.

"Has your friend had any chemotherapy?" Arch asked, from the foot of the bed.

"What's chemotherapy? Never mind. I wouldn't know if you told me. He's had the best treatment money could buy, I can tell you that. But he's still sick. Now I figure it like this. My union has some money in the bank. We been building up what we call a sick fund. The boys agree with me that nobody can afford to be sick any more, and we get a lot of men off the job, with one thing and another. Some of the load is carried by insurance, sure. But who's got enough—having kids, sending 'em to school, sometimes having a sick wife—that he can pay even the difference between what the insurance allows and what these joints clip you for?" The restless right hand was a fist, now, the knuckles white against the coverlet.

"I've been in here three weeks, and already I've spent more'n a thousand dollars. That doesn't include any for you guys," he said to Arch. "None of my boys could afford that. I figure it's good business to go along with those fellows in this cancer deal." Susan and Arch again exchanged glances. Excited was the way Susan felt, and Arch was pulling at his right ear, a sure sign of his being emotionally involved.

Cox was speaking again.

"Make a note, Miss Farley, to ask Doc Mitchell for an appointment for my friend Barney Hopkins. I think he better come down here where you folks will treat him like a person. Too many sick men up there, and he's gotten to be a file folder full of X-ray pictures to those birds."

Susan made the memorandum.

"Then call this number in Washington and ask for the balance in the sick fund account." He gave Susan the number, and she stood by the bed and put in the call over the room telephone.

"How much you figure it would cost to build a research laboratory here at St. Patrick's and install a staff of cancer experts to look people over–" Arch murmured, "diagnose," and Cox swept on. "Then treat 'em with whatever they decide is best. And I don't want it too big. I want the people who come here to be–" The strong voice hesitated, and then the black eyes lighted up. "I want 'em to be treated like Oliver Cox has been. A human being in a lot of trouble. When it grows too big–St. Patrick's, I mean–for people to be people, then my boys' money can go on to some other hospital that can use it."

The number in Washington was ringing. When a man's voice answered, Susan handed the telephone to Cox.

"Would you like us to leave?" Arch asked.

The pepper-and-salt crew cut nodded curtly.

Susan and Arch went into the hall.

"This could be the biggest thing that ever happened to St. Patrick's–and to us," Arch said, when they were outside the closed door.

"I'm so excited I've got goose bumps," Susan said, rubbing her arm.

Dr. Mitchell and the bone specialist in charge of Oliver Cox's case came down the hall toward Room 212.

In 214, there was a boy with two broken legs, one in traction, the other in a cast. He habitually watched television on the portable set his parents had installed on the chest of drawers beyond the foot of his bed. He switched it on and off at will, from a control he kept mostly in his hand. When Susan and Arch came out into the hall, the television was noisily broadcasting a soap opera. Apparently the young patient tired of the sufferings of the characters, for abruptly he switched off the set.

The resultant silence failed to mask the conversation of the two doctors, now almost to where Arch and Susan waited for Cox to finish his telephone conversation. What they heard made Susan's face crimson again.

"—clumsy, stupid fool of a nurse broke the pitcher, then left it on the floor; of course I put my foot in it." Dr. Mitchell was explaining his bandaged right hand. To do him credit, Susan supposed he hadn't expected the television to be cut off, if he'd been conscious of it in the first place. Had Dr. Mitchell known she was there? She didn't look, to see. She lowered her eyes and stepped aside for the two doctors to go in, after a casual knock. Arch replied to their greeting, and commented that Cox was on the telephone. But the two men went in, anyway.

"I'd like to go home," Susan said miserably.

"Don't start feeling sorry for yourself," Arch told her bluntly. "Nothing's different from what it was half an hour ago, except that you're the key person in a project that might bring a greal deal of relief to a great many people. Including your father."

"How sympathetic you are, Doctor." Susan gave him a sidewise look from her deeply blue eyes. Her dimple showed briefly. Arch was right, of course. Impulsively, she put a hand on his white-coated arm and gave it a quick pat.

"What's that for?" he asked, his brown eyes smiling.

"For keeping me on the beam," she told him. "Come to supper tonight—I won't give you scrambled eggs," she promised.

"I can't come," Arch said regretfully. "I've got something else on. I'd a lot rather go to the Farleys' for supper, though, than to the Country Club." From the tone of his voice, he really was sorry. And Susan's quick mind knew without asking that Arch would be taking Mavis Pennington to the weekly dinner dance at the Palm City Country Club.

"Another time, then," she said pleasantly. She really did want to go home, now. She said so, adding that she was making a party dress for Grace, and it had to be finished for the same dance to which Arch was going. "I've got at least an hour and a half's work on it," she commented. "If it isn't ready, the poor kid'll collapse. I should have worked on it the night we went swimming."

Arch drew his dark brows together in a frown.

Susan thought, *Does he think I meant to remind him about the shark, for goodness' sake?* No man wanted to be pulled out of the water by a girl, and then reminded of it every breath. Arch had thanked her for saving his life, that night before he went home, and they hadn't discussed it since, although there had been stories in the paper about an infestation of sharks at the local beaches, driven closer than usual inshore by the warmth of the water.

I never will learn to think before I speak, Susan thought. Aloud, she said, "He can't be talking this long. And with Dr. Mitchell there, and his own doctor, there's no telling when he'll be wanting me again. I just haven't got the *time*, Arch. You stay–you can tell him twice as much as I can, and after all, he only wanted me to make notes."

"You do as you wish, Susan." Arch, Susan thought, sounded a little remote. But he didn't look that way. She met his brown gaze in a long look that held. Inwardly, she felt all the trouble melting. "I'll explain," he promised.

All the way home, she remembered the way he'd looked at her. Surely Arch didn't look at Mavis Pennington that way.

Susan didn't want to go to the Country Club dinner dance, not even when Grace was dressed and admiring herself in the full-length mirror. The yards and yards of crisp organdie, with its deep hem to hold it against the many layers of nylon-net petticoats, and the tiny gathers snugged into Grace's slim waist, made Susan's sister look like the girl in the magazine whose picture Susan had used as a model for making the dress. A narrow periwinkle velvet ribbon, looped into a bow, was just the right note of contrast.

Grace kissed Susan and pulled her to the door to meet her escort, the latest object of Grace's unstable affections. "His father is that real estate man who's building that big new subdivision," Grace told Susan. "He's got loads of money, or he couldn't do all that developing." Susan said nothing about the money's belonging to Dr. Christopher Mitchell. She was thinking, watching Grace and her escort drive off, that it took a whole lot of lip-cancer cases like that poor creature in the dentist's office to build a subdivision. Then she smothered such unprofessional ideas, and picked up the evening paper from the steps.

Her father was having his before-dinner nap. She had a few minutes before taking the meat loaf out of the oven. So she sat down on the divan in the pleasant living room and put her tired feet on a convenient hassock. Unfolding the paper, she was astonished to see her own face, beneath its hospital cap, looking at her. It was her graduation picture; all the girls in her class had had them taken by the studio, and a feature-story writer had used the individual pictures to point up an article on St. Patrick's Nursing School.

"Local Nurse Stages Second Rescue of Summer," the headlines read. The story was an account of Susan's assistance to Arch in the shark affair. Where had the paper gotten it? Susan was physically sick. She and Arch had agreed to say nothing about it. There was a paragraph about Pamela Durrance, and Susan's part in that affair. And a repetition of the warning about sharks. The whole thing was handled as a part of the paper's campaign to make the beaches safer for swimmers, it was stated.

Al Duffy wasn't going to like this tie-in of the hospital in what was sure to be regarded as unfavorable publicity. And the use of Susan's picture in nursing uniform—it couldn't be much worse.

CHAPTER X

The unhappiness that Susan had felt at Arch's attentions to Mavis Pennington was as nothing compared to what she suffered after the shark story was released. She'd understood, in a way, that the girl in the pink pinafore was a part of Christopher Mitchell's domination over the young interns and residents of St. Patrick's. Several of the others were pressed into service from time to time, and Susan had a healthy and pretty girl's inner superiority over dates that were duty dates.

"But she's got plenty on the ball," Susan admitted to herself on the way to the hospital the next morning. "Any girl would be crazy not to be wary of competition like that. But that is normal, ordinary competition. What can I do to ease the hurt this story is going to cause Arch? The other fellows are going to rib him about being both shark bait and woman bait—I can just hear them."

She had it all fixed in her mind what she would say to Arch. She knew he would be on Second, East, to call on Oliver Cox, sometime during the morning.

A new case had come down from Surgery, for Second, East, however, and Susan was forced to keep a close eye on her. The attending doctor had come in on the heels of the guerney that brought the patient, an automobile accident victim.

"It was one of those unnecessary, avoidable things," he told Susan. "This girl will be lucky if we save her leg."

"Oh, no!" Involuntarily, Susan winced.

"She's nauseated," the doctor said. "Vomited pretty badly in the recovery room. Maybe she'll be all right now. We'll watch her closely, eh?" He was one of the older doctors, and Susan liked him.

"Yes, sir," she promised. He stood looking down at the girl on the bed, and the great gray eyes opened and the girl tried to smile.

"Hi, Doc," she said clearly, and was immediately asleep again.

"See what I mean? Courage. She knows the possibilities. As a matter of fact, she thought the leg was gone when I met her in Emergency."

"What happened? Have you time, sir—?" Susan's recent experience with Dr. Mitchell had made her very tentative with doctors.

"She was driving her car downtown, and her sister was with her. The sister's outside now in the lounge. I'm going to talk to her in a minute. Girl's hysterical herself, and small wonder. That's a terrible leg. Bone crushed, flesh mangled. Senseless. Absolutely senseless." He cleared his throat and wiped his glasses. Susan waited, her eyes on the I.V. that dripped into the veins of the sleeping girl.

"She got out of the car, and the sister slid over under the wheel. It seems the sister stepped on the gas, instead of the brake. A common admittance ticket to St. Patrick's," the old man said gloomily. "At any rate, the car lurched forward, and this one was pinned between it and a parked car. Stayed that way for five minutes, screaming. Sister couldn't drive forward nor backward to release her. Had to stay there. Does something to the brain, that kind of thing. Considerable shock."

Susan felt the horror and sympathy like a physical blow. "What then?" she asked.

"Truckload of men drove by, stopped and lifted the two cars apart. Ambulance there by then."

"Will she be all right?"

"Depends on how clean the metal was on those two cars."

"Will she need specials?"

"It would help," the doctor said drily. "No one on the register. Not even a licensed practical nurse, except a male orderly who wouldn't exactly do. No, it's up to you, Nurse." He left, to talk to the inconsolable sister.

It wasn't until nearly noon that Susan had an opportunity to put her head into Room 212.

"Look at us," Amy greeted her. "We're out of traction!"

Oliver Cox smiled at her from the bed, even though there was a white line of pain around the thin lips. "I'm demobilized for sure, now," he said. "This member," nodding at his hand, a swollen, puffy thing that lay helplessly on the coverlet, "is acting up."

Arch came in then.

"Hello, this morning," he said cheerfully. "I hear you're out of harness." The weights were on the dresser. Arch picked one up, and held it, idly hefting it. Then he put it down, and went over to the bed. He had not yet acknowledged Susan's presence. He did so now, including her and Amy in an impersonal "good morning."

Amy's eyebrows shot up, and she met Susan's eye.

"I see you two collaborated to crash the front page," Cox commented, covering up the pain that must be racking him as Arch examined the swollen hand and wrist, caused by returned circulation and the removal of the wire.

"Yeah." Arch touched the wrist with gentle fingers. "So I hear." He did not look at Susan.

Susan dropped her eyelids to hide the quick pain in her heart. It wasn't possible that Arch realized how this would hurt her, in front of two people who knew what good friends they were.

"Excuse me," she said, and left them, Arch with his dark head bent over the patient's arm, Amy big-eyed with knowledge that there was something going on, and Cox gray-faced with pain, but thanking her with his dark eyes for coming in.

Susan went in automatically to tone down the television in Room 214. The boy with the broken legs wanted a Coke. Susan got it for him.

She looked in again on the girl in Room 220, more rational now, and wanting water. Susan went for crushed ice. Tenderly, she held it in a spoon, to the beautiful lips.

"Pain," the girl said, long lashes against pale cheeks.

"We'll do something for that, just as soon as we can," Susan promised.

"Sick," the girl murmured, and Susan attended to that, too. This girl should have someone with her.

Susan went on quiet feet to the desk. "Mrs. Freeman, I believe two-twenty needs someone there; she is nauseated and very restless," she reported.

"I don't know what we can do—" The old woman was harassed by mounting worries. Being short-handed was a floor supervisor's nightmare. "O'Hara's husband is sick and she couldn't come to work; an aide didn't show up. There's no possible help to be had from the registry. I'll just have to phone Mrs. Branch to send us someone." She picked up the phone and asked for the Director of Nursing Services. A short one-sided conversation ensued. Susan didn't wait to hear what excuse Mrs. Branch would make; there actually was an acute shortage of help throughout the hospital; she'd been hearing about it for days—in the cafeteria, in the halls, and at the time-card racks where the staff punched in and out.

When she was near the desk again, on her way to the kitchen to get hot water for a cup of bouillon for a nervous patient, Mrs. Freeman called to her.

"Himself—Mr. Duffy—would like to see you in his office," she told Susan. For a wonder, she offered no further comment, and Susan was grateful for small favors. She supposed "old Mrs. Little America," as Cox called her, was too immersed in her own difficulties to add to Susan's.

But when Susan walked into Himself's office, she knew she was in for it. Ordinarily, Mrs. Branch was the one to discipline nurses. This would be something more serious. Susan squared her shoulders and lifted her chin.

"Sit down, Miss Farley," the Administrator invited.

"Thank you." Susan sat, and looked down into nowhere, properly respectful.

"You know I made a point of keeping you at St. Patrick's," Duffy began. "I believed you had the makings of a fine nurse."

Susan's eyes flew wide open. Was Al Duffy going to question her professional ability? She was on the verge of saying that her scoring at graduation was the top of the class, but restrained herself. Let Himself do the talking.

"You know in a place like this we have to have something besides professional proficiency," he went on. "We have to get along together. I've had nothing but a hornet's nest of trouble ever since you graduated." His very blue eyes were troubled. Susan realized he was far from enjoying this interview. It somehow helped her own control.

"The strange part of it is," the Irishman continued, "it doesn't ever seem to be anything you could have helped doing. Nothing, that is, except this last thing." He gave the newspaper on his desk a distasteful push. "It's bad taste, Susan, and I'm surprised at you."

Susan, at first only worried and frightened, was by now furiously angry. All her self-control of the past few months, the lock on her tongue to keep herself from saying what she thought, all the "womanly docility" the Sister in charge of the conduct class had stressed, flew out of the window.

"I grieve at your poor opinion of me, sir," she said, her voice a pleasant, conversational tone. Hearing herself, she thought that the words seemed to be coming from someone else, and that she, herself, was mentally slapping all the orderly stacks of paper from Himself's desk.

Duffy grew redder in the face than he ordinarily was, which was considerable. His hair looked three shades whiter, by contrast, and his eyes four shades bluer. "Don't say anything you'll be sorry for," he sputtered.

"You know," Susan straightened the folds of her poplin skirt, which didn't need it, "when I was capped," a slender-fingered hand gave the wisp of organdie on her head a light fillip, "I thought that to work in this hospital was the beginning and end of all happiness for me. Maybe it still is; but I must say it has cost me loss of face, loss of personal pride, loss of the kind of work I wanted so terribly to do, and now, loss of my ideas of your sense of justice, Mr. Duffy."

She thought the Administrator was going to have a stroke. "*My* sense of justice?" His Irish accent made it sound like "Moi since of juice-tice."

"I didn't give that story to the paper, you know. You didn't even ask me." Susan was quieter now.

"You needn't add falsehood to the score." The Administrator's feelings had been hurt. And his own control, never too good, had suffered.

Susan rose to the full height of her five feet four inches. Her raised chin tilted the red chignon against the slender column of her neck, and she looked very young and vulnerable.

"I'm not a liar, Mr. Duffy," she said stiffly, suddenly frightened again at the knowledge that now her resignation was inevitable. What would they do? Dad sick, Grace making a good attempt to study under limited financial conditions, and Susan without a job.

But how could she stay, under the circumstances? They didn't want her here. Her throat constricted, and there was the old familiar sting of tears behind her eyes. Well, she wasn't going to cry, not here, anyway.

"But I can at least relieve you of the necessity to stand up against Dr. Mitchell any longer. I should have known I couldn't buck his animosity." She turned to go. There was a deep carpet in this room. Her feet hardly touched it, so swiftly did she make her way to the door.

Once there, however, it occurred to her that it would make sense to ask one more question. "Mr. Duffy, why are you so sure I'm not telling the truth?"

"Why, I called the paper, of course. The city desk told

me one of his reporters had gotten the story from you. He verified it, while I held the phone."

Susan's jaw dropped. So she, herself, had been unjust to Mr. Duffy. She leaned her tired shoulders against the mahogany panel of the door, and sighed.

"Well, I'm very sorry I was rude. But I must, I suppose, let my resignation stand. I can't continue to embarrass St. Patrick's, since, as you say, things seem to happen in my wake. 'Accident prone,' perhaps, if there is such a thing, and our psychology instructor assured us there is. Good night, Mr. Duffy."

Did professional ethics demand that she go back to Second, East, and tell Mrs. Freeman? Susan, feeling that the world had fallen away from her feet, made herself go back upstairs.

The short minute it took the self-service elevator to ascend the one floor seemed forever. Susan wanted to get home where she could shut the door of her room and think this thing out. Or just lick her wounds.

Instead, when she got to the desk, an involuntary look down the hall showed that every light was on. And Mrs. Freeman wasn't there. Susan went to the light of the girl in Room 220. She would never know why, when there were others nearer.

Susan's practiced eye went first to the I.V. bottle. How long since she'd been in here? An hour? Two hours? The fluid level in the bottle had not lowered appreciably, not so that she could tell any had gone into the girl's vein. Susan checked the needle at the girl's wrist, not an easy thing to do, for the patient was flailing around in the bed. Her teeth were chattering, her lips blue.

Swiftly, Susan got the two blankets from the closet shelf, and put them over the girl. Next she raised the sides of the bed so that the patient wouldn't fall out. Then she gently assured the girl that everything was under control.

With one last, concerned look at the ugly look of the arm where the fluid had scattered among the tissues, she ran for the desk.

This time, Mrs. Freeman was there.

"Thank heaven you're here," Susan said in a low voice. "The girl in two-twenty is in shock. Her I.V. wasn't in the vein, I guess. Anyway, she's having convulsions."

Mrs. Freeman, though crabbed and prejudiced, was a good nurse. She had matters under control in seconds. Susan went on to attend to the other lights, doing what was necessary.

She almost forgot about Al Duffy and her world-shattering interview. Almost, but not quite.

Three o'clock came in a rush. She never did get to say goodbye to Mrs. Freeman, nor, she realized after she was almost home, to Oliver Cox.

CHAPTER XI

The car parked in the Farley driveway, Susan was confronted with the problem of what to tell her family.

She got as far as the cement steps, and lowered herself down to the second from the top. This was where she'd stood, thinking that she could be as tall as Arch if he stood on the ground and she on this step. It was as good a place as any to take stock.

It was one of those late summer afternoons that make northwest Florida the vacation paradise for all of Alabama, and much of Mississippi and Georgia. Susan looked upward at the remote blueness of the sky, and wondered if those unseen planets in the unknown galaxies fostered troubles like hers. "Just about every kind of trouble—you name 'em, I've got 'em," she addressed them. Her father's precarious health, Grace's education, her own job trouble. And now, this rift between her and Arch.

Off toward the west, there was a totally white cloud formation, the stratospheric winds having molded them to look the way sand does on the floor of the sea. The beauty of the day began to lift Susan's spirits somewhat. The reflection of the westering sunlight against the pavement made itself felt on her sensitive skin, and with a thought to the resultant freckles that were sure to follow, she told herself she should go inside. Lethargy, and dread of facing her father now, made her stall for a few more moments.

The city bus stopped at the corner and Grace got off. Susan watched her sister come toward her, thinking that eighteen was a wonderful age. Free of the doubts and fears of childhood, free, too, of the responsibilities and misgivings that would come with maturity. *She's really beautiful, with that dark hair and magnolia complexion,* Susan thought, feeling her heart swell with love.

"Hi!" Grace called when she was within a few yards of her sister. "Nice, cool spot you picked for yourself there."

"I got this far and collapsed," Susan confessed.

"You got away this morning before I had a chance to tell you what a divine time I had in that Cloud Nine of a dress you made." Grace stopped on the walk at the foot of the steps and struck a pose that was an exaggerated model stance. "I was the belle of the ball," she sighed happily. "Come on in; I'll fix you a glass of iced tea."

Susan felt a bit of reflected pleasure from the younger girl's mood. Sometimes it had been less than gratifying sewing for Grace, having her take for granted the long hours at the machine, the basting, fitting, cutting. Maybe her sister was growing up.

"That'll be swell. But sit down a moment; I have news, and I don't want to break it to Dad until after you and I have a chance to talk."

"Well, at least let's sit in the swing." Grace dropped her books on the old couch with the faded green cover. It was shady on the east end of the porch. The swing was an ancient wooden affair, hung on chains from rusted iron eyes. It creaked and complained whenever anyone used it. This had been the favorite evening resting place of their mother.

The couch was Dad's, Susan was remembering. It was saddening to see it dusty and sagging with neglect. She made a mental resolution to use some of her new enforced leisure to make a couch cover and swing cushions, and make him spend some time out there.

Where to start? Susan made an effort to gather her thoughts, a jumble of Oliver Cox and his plan for a research-treatment cancer center at St. Patrick's, Al Duffy's accusation, Mrs. Freeman's continued coolness; Dr. Mitchell's animosity; Arch's defection. And the dull ache of financial insecurity. She blurted out the worst at once:

"I had to quit my job at the hospital."

Grace stopped swinging abruptly. "You're kidding!"

"No laughing matter," Susan said grimly. "I guess I just wasn't intended to work at St. Patrick's. In a way, it's all my fault." This was a new point of view. Talking about it brought things into sharper focus. She went on. "I should never have promised to work for Dr. Mitchell if I didn't intend to go through with it. That was the beginning of all my trouble."

"But we thought—" Grace began.

"We thought it would be worth the money. *I* thought, that is. And then I didn't think so. I let him count on me, then I pulled the rug out from under his feet." Susan remembered that she had offered to fill in until he had someone else. But why should he break in two new nurses? Bad enough to train one. There was certainly something to be said for Dr. Mitchell's point of view.

"I humiliated him by accepting another job over his head. And then I caused him that hand injury—an unforgivable crime for a nurse. And all the time, did I ever once try to make him understand?" Susan compressed her lips. No wonder she was out of a job.

"What will you do?"

"Something will work out, I guess. But the thing that hurts me most is Arch." She told Grace about Oliver Cox, his plan for the cancer program, in which she would have had a part, with Arch. "I don't see how I could help, but Mr. Cox apparently had it all worked out in his mind."

"You just walked out of there and didn't *ask* him?" Grace was incredulous.

"Arch was in his room, and Dr. Mitchell and another doctor. . . . And after that, I was too busy." Susan was thinking of the girl with the crushed leg.

"How did Dr. Mitchell sell a bill of goods to Arch? I'd have bet my last dollar that Arch makes his own decisions, forms his own opinions." Grace looked indignant.

"Oh, I didn't make it clear. It wasn't Dr. Mitchell that caused Arch to be remote. It was Al Duffy and the story in the paper about the shark."

"Oh, was it in? I didn't have a chance to look," Grace said excitedly. "I meant to, the first thing this morning." She jumped up and started in to look for the paper, then stopped abruptly. "What did you say? The *paper* caused all this?" Bewilderment, disbelief, contrition followed themselves across her mobile face in quick succession.

"The hospital seems to think I used my job there to get myself a little personal publicity," Susan said drily. "I don't understand how they got the information in the first place. There absolutely wasn't anyone on that beach but Arch and me, and I didn't tell anyone but you."

Grace was sitting on the couch now, looking at Susan with enormous brown eyes that swam in tears. Suddenly Susan understood.

"I did it," Grace said, gulping in the middle of a word. The tears spilled over the long dark lashes and rolled down her cheeks. She buried her face in her hands, so that Susan had difficulty in understanding what she said. "I told this boy who works on the paper. He's in my English class, and works part time—and was covering that thing about the sharks. I t-t-told him about you. I was so p-p-proud . . ." Grace was sobbing now, great, racking sobs that shook her slim body. She fell over on her face, her books sliding unnoticed to the floor.

"Don't cry, Grace." Susan, her own distress forgotten, knelt on the floor by the couch to comfort her sister. "It doesn't matter that much." She gathered the shaking girl into her arms, and put the disheveled head on her shoulder. Gently, she rocked her sister back and forth, kneeling there by the dusty old cot. She hadn't comforted Grace like this since she was too small to come up the steps by herself.

And she must have had heartaches that needed comforting, Susan thought. *What makes people who love each other let a glass wall come between them?* Aloud, she said practically, "Dad will hear you, lamb, and I can't rock you both."

Grace stopped instantly. She hunted around for a tissue in her pocket. Finding it, she blew her nose vigorously.

"Come on," she said.

"What?" Susan looked blank. Grace had started down the steps, instead of into the house.

"Come on. Just like you are. Just like I am—and I'm a mess. I can fix my face in the car."

"No doubt," Susan agreed. "But where are we going?"

"To see that man. That Mr. Duffy. I'm going to tell him I was the Miss Farley who told the reporter about the shark, and then you can stay quit or not, as you like. But he's going to know it." Susan was backing the car out of the driveway.

It actually didn't matter as much about St. Patrick's as it did that Grace was taking the initiative to remedy what she had done. Somehow, Susan felt that all the heartache of the past months wasn't in vain; it had brought her close to Grace. In a rare gesture of affection, she reached over and gave her sister's hand a quick squeeze.

"Don't be nice to me right now," Grace said with shaky laughter. "I might cry again—and I'm not crying in front of that man."

"That man" was busy when the two girls entered the Administrator's quarters. The outer office was presided over by Eunice Coates, who had been here when Susan was in training. "Himself has a delegation in there," Eunice explained. "Won't you wait?"

"Yes, we will." Grace took the initiative. "And where would I find Dr. Curtis at this hour?"

The receptionist met Susan's eye, and managed not to look surprised.

Susan answered her sister, understanding that it was Grace's wish to kill two birds with one stone. "You look on the board and see if he's in the building," she explained. "Then you get the communications desk to put in a call for him."

Grace came back, beaming. "He's coming," she announced.

The door to Aloysius Duffy's office opened, and a group of men came out, all talking excitedly. Himself, Susan saw, was using his desk telephone. He caught sight of her in the anteroom. Did his face brighten? She wasn't sure. Then the door closed behind the last of the departing visitors.

"Your little sister has grown up," the receptionist remarked.

"I was just noticing," Susan agreed.

Grace grinned. "High time, too."

The mahogany door jerked open the second time. Himself boomed like a trumpeting elephant: "Come in here!"

The sisters went in together.

"Mr. Duffy, I told the reporter about Susan and the shark," Grace said before Susan could introduce her. Her look was one of "get it over with."

Himself made a gesture with one huge hand, almost knocking the telephone from the corner of the big desk.

"A detail," he said, his blue eyes dancing. "You saved me the trouble of sending for this one." He wagged his leonine head at Susan. "I'm not letting you resign, though Mrs. Freeman's lost a good nurse," he said. He flipped the switch of his intercom and waited impatiently for the girl outside to acknowledge his need of her. There was silence in the room.

Susan and Grace looked at each other. The Administrator's color deepened. His voice rumbled in the nether regions of his chest. "Eunice!" The great bellow shook the slats of the Venetian blind. Grace jumped, and Susan got up and opened the door. The outside room was empty.

"It's five o'clock, sir," she said, noticing the hands on the big wall clock.

"Clock watchers. Nothing but clock watchers in this hospital. Run out of here like water down the drain." The Irish accent seemed to deepen. "Wanted her to get Curtis in here."

"He's coming," Grace said brightly.

"Eh?" Himself blinked at this unexpected co-operation.

Arch obliged by making his entrance into the outside office at that moment. Susan hadn't closed the inside office door, so he came directly in. As he walked past her, there was a sort of bruised unhappiness in his brown eyes.

"Got a correction, first off," Al Duffy told the young resident. "Told you a lie. Believed it myself. Wrong Miss Farley spilled the beans." The man's blue eyes darted from one to the other. "Tempest in a teapot. Wrong to let Mitchell get me all worked up. Sit down, Curtis." With understandable bewilderment, Arch sat. He tried not to look at Susan, did look, and was unable to look anywhere else.

"Cox's Executive Committee just flew in from Washington," Himself announced. "They held a meeting here in my office, and they're on their way upstairs to tell him his plan is approved. There's a whole ball full of strings attached, though." The huge hand ruffled the white hair distractedly.

"Strings?" Arch echoed.

"The darnedest strings you ever heard of. First, we got us a baby to raise. Cox wants young Pat Durrance to be the hospital's baby, and we fix him up a suite for his home —Cox, of course, to pay for the fixin'." Mr. Duffy stopped to consider the strange ways of sick men. "He's setting up a trust fund for schooling and whatever. He's put me through the hoop with the Welfare people. They won't take kindly to the hospital's having a baby." Duffy wiped the considerable expanse of sweating brow with an immaculate handkerchief.

"Then, soon as the new wing is completed, Dr. Curtis is to work with the best cancer man they can find, probably someone from New York. And you, Nurse Farley—you're to be some kind of combined Florence Nightingale and Madame Curie, I couldn't quite understand which." The Administrator stopped and took a shaken breath. "As for me, I'm only the fellow who works out all the impossible details." He caught sight of Grace, and looked at her admiringly.

"Where does *she* fit into this crazy scheme?" Himself seemed to think it was a day for making room for all comers.

"I don't, sir; I'm learning to teach school," Grace replied primly. "If you'll excuse me, I might say I like things logical and orderly. This wouldn't do for me *at all!*" She gave a sort of wave, and turned to leave. "Susan?"

"Would you let me bring her along?" Arch asked Grace, without looking away from Susan.

Susan handed Grace the keys to the car.

"Not for awhile, Curtis," Himself said firmly. "Cox wants to see Susan in two-twelve right away."

Without understanding how it worked out that way, Susan was on her way back to Second, East, and Arch's long legs were taking him away from her in the opposite direction. But the look he'd given her was enough to sustain the in-between time. "All time away from him is in-between time," Susan told herself, turning the familiar corner into the long corridor where the light was on over Room 212.

CHAPTER XII

Oliver Cox was sitting up in a chair.

Susan had never seen so resplendent a robe as was tied snugly around his narrow waist. It was made of some sort of metallic fabric, and above its barbaric effect, the very black eyes of Oliver Cox suggested something of the power of an Eastern potentate. His short hair was freshly cut, and he was obviously freshly shaven. The prophylactic smell of the hospital room was replaced by the more characteristic one for Oliver Cox of expensive after-shave lotion.

"I hear you quit," he greeted Susan. "Sit down."

"Against the rules," Susan reminded him.

"But you don't work here any more," he countered, the black eyes glinting with humor.

"I'll stand," Susan said easily. "How's the arm?"

"Lousy," Cox answered, looking with disfavor at the muslin sling issued by Central Supplies. "Look, Miss Farley—Susan—will you do an errand for me? I'd like a couple or so black silk squares, like ladies wear for scarfs, to use for this sling routine. I don't like the looks of this cloth."

Susan smiled an affirmative.

"The big Irishman says he's going to put you on a sort of special duty, while things get under way for the cancer clinic. You know about the cancer clinic?" If a man could swagger while he was sitting in a deep armchair, Oliver Cox swaggered. "The teamsters and the auto fellows are going to flip when they get a load of what we're doing," he gloated.

Susan asked when he expected his project to get under way, and he waved his good hand in a dismissal of time.

"I rolled down the hall to have a look at the hospital's baby," Cox told her seriously. "He's quite a boy. I think he's a lot like both of 'em." There was quiet for a few seconds. "What do you think of a baby having a hospital for its folks?"

Susan didn't answer right away. It was so apparent that Oliver Cox thought he'd found a perfect solution for all the ills of his world that Susan hesitated to give an honest answer. But he wasn't having any holding out. "All right, all right, so you don't think much of it?" The thin lips showed his disappointment.

"Well, I think it is wonderful of you to provide for the baby, and of course Palm City is a wonderful place for a boy to grow up—he can be a part of the outdoor world as he never could in the North. But do you feel that a hospital is the right environment for a growing child? Wouldn't you rather a real family had him? A husband and wife who, having no children of their own, would give him the love and affection his own parents can't?"

"Yeah. That's what I mean." The thin lips didn't relax. "Couples fight between themselves. The best of 'em. Like his own mother and father. They loved each other so much they couldn't stand living if it wasn't just right. Naw—I want to prove something." The clean-shaven chin was set stubbornly.

"Now let's talk about something else important." He leaned forward in his chair. "Barney Hopkins will be here tomorrow, and Doc Curtis and Doc Mitchell are going to look him over. He's coming straight to the hospital. Would it be asking too much for you to kind of take Alice Hopkins under your wing? She's going to be lost, away from their kids, and off down here."

"I'd love to." Susan was glad to be able to promise something. She felt that not being enthusiastic about Cox's plan for Pat Durrance was perhaps cruel at this point, but she had a feeling about it. And it was no use trying to hide it, not from those boring eyes, which seemed to see through anything but truth.

"I must run," she told the man in the easy chair. His face fell. *Why*, Susan thought with surprise, *he's acting like a child—I guess illness makes them all boys.* "Thanks for everything," she said aloud, and slipped out before Cox could make it difficult. The picture of him, dressed in that ridiculous robe, all slicked up by the hospital barber, the long evening ahead of him without prospect of family or friends dropping in, was with Susan until she got downstairs. Then her mind turned to thoughts of her own evening.

She paused to telephone home. Grace answered, her young voice clear and purposeful. "I knew it would be you," she said. "Arch phoned, and left a message. He said for you to be ready by eight for a special evening, and it wasn't going to be any box supper."

"Goodness, what'll I wear?" Susan worried aloud.

"I've pressed your blue linen," Grace said. "I'd come get

you, but I don't think I'd better leave Dad. Hop a cab and come on."

"Is he worse?" Susan's heart gave a lurch.

"N-n-no, but he's gone into his room a bit earlier than usual. I guess he's tired." Grace obviously didn't want a cloud over Susan's evening. Susan felt a rush of affection for her sister. For Grace to press a dress for Susan was front-page.

In spite of herself, Susan found herself humming an old song under her breath. It had been around a long time—she couldn't quite remember what it was, only the haunting sweetness of the melody. She stood on the front steps of the hospital, and the offshore wind tugged briskly at her skirts, then rumpled the smoothness of her dark-red hair, as she waited for her cab.

The Spanish moss in the huge old live oak that grew in the center of the curving driveway blew toward her, and the waves slapped against the bay bulkhead in time to Susan's song. Without realizing it, the words had injected themselves into her mind. "—I'll get by, as long as I have you," she sang under her breath. The cab drove up and stopped. She got in, gave her directions, and leaned back against the seat, a slim girl in a white uniform, with a lot of auburn hair that seemed almost too heavy for the slender neck to carry.

Tonight Susan was going to banish from her mind all thoughts of the sprawling building behind her. *I sometimes think it's a tentacled monster that reaches its shining waxed corridors into the crevices of our lives*, she mused. *And we are Pygmies that can't combat it. But I'm going to combat it tonight*, she promised herself, as the cab let her out at home.

Grace had filled the old-fashioned tub with water that was almost tepid. "No cold shower for you, my girl," she said, pushing Susan toward the bathroom. "You have just enough time to soak for fifteen minutes. I'm fixing you a cup of tea." The tea was what made tears come to Susan's eyes. It was their mother's antidote for life's pressures.

Susan almost went to sleep against the slanting end of the tub. She hardly heard Grace's knock on the door. "Time's up," her sister announced.

Susan gave herself a brisk rubbing, thinking that the bathroom, with its make-up gear atop the old painted chest of drawers that held towels, washcloths, medical supplies, and hot-water bottle, its faded linoleum floor, its single light bulb at the end of a drop cord, was a museum piece. In the wintertime the single flooring was icy-cold to bare feet, and the board-and-batten wall of the added-on rectangle admitted shafts of sunlight through weathered cracks.

But I couldn't feel more rested if I'd bathed in the marble pools of the Romans, Susan thought. In terry-cloth robe, she was ready for her tea.

Grace, at the breakfast-alcove table, was poring over her lessons for tomorrow. "Tests," she announced, moving the books aside to make room for Susan's tea. "And that reminds me," she gave Susan an admonishing look. "You have it out with Arch about that Pennington dame. She leans on him as if she owns him—well," Grace reconsidered, "anyway as if she had a ninety-year lease."

Susan laughed. "She does that to all the fellows." But she wished she and Arch were independent of Christopher Mitchell and his favors. If she were ever to work with Arch, it would have to be through Dr. Mitchell's permission, for Himself would never override the Chief of Staff twice. Then she brushed that from her mind. Tonight, she wouldn't worry about Mavis Pennington, or Surgery, either.

She went into her room, where the blue linen sheath was laid out on the bed. "Come in with me while I dress," she called to Grace.

"You're getting too thin," Grace commented, observing the fit of her sister's slip.

"It's just as well." Susan pulled the blue linen over her head and Grace zipped it up the back. Its close-fitting lines followed the curves of Susan's figure with a wrinkle-free closeness that would have been spoiled by an additional ounce of weight on the part of its wearer.

Susan had arranged her hair in a new way, pulling the soft auburn waves down over her ears, but carrying the bulk of the chignon up to the crown of her head. A few tendrils escaped the arrangement and curled tightly at the nape of her neck. Grace, noticing them, said nothing, thinking it added softness and femininity.

At the last minute, she ran into her room and came back with her own pink pearl earrings. The great globes made Susan's ears look very small, and her darkly blue eyes very large.

It was well past dark when Arch came. "Don't put on the porch light," Grace cautioned. Susan laughed at such elaborate stage setting, but she went down the steps in the light from the car lamps.

Arch opened the car door for her, and held her briefly before letting her get inside. Neither spoke.

In the light from the dash, Susan could see that his jaw was set sternly, the way it always was when he was thinking in the single-purpose way he had.

Arch spoke first.

"The Chateau," he said distinctly.

Susan, inside the happy place that was her mind, had been humming the melody that had haunted her all evening.

"Are we rich?" she asked contentedly.

"For the moment. Not after." Arch gave a sudden chortle that was good to hear. "It's worth the usurious interest Jimmy Camp will take out of my hide." Jimmy Camp was one of St. Patrick's interns who had used his terminal Army pay to get up a nest egg that had hatched many a festive evening for fellow staff doctors.

"Arch, we haven't talked for a long time. Are you going into this clinic thing Oliver Cox has dreamed up for St. Patrick's?"

"It looks good," Arch said slowly. "He's actually gotten Hubbard to come down from New York; to agree to, that is," he added. Hubbard was the beginning and end of all surgical experts in the cancer field, to Arch. To Susan, too. She had read avidly everything Hubbard had ever written in the medical papers. She began to feel excitement rushing into her veins.

"God bless Oliver Cox," she said.

"Sure," Arch agreed. "But while I don't grudge him the bounty of the Almighty, I'd feel better about it if he hadn't tied it all up with that baby."

"There's one thing about it," Susan commented, as they pulled into the parking area of the town's most elaborate beach establishment. "I just don't believe you'd be happiest as a clinician forever, Arch."

"You think I'm the private-practice type, like Doc Mitchell?" Arch was laughing at her.

"Not exactly." Susan wasn't to be diverted. "But I can't see you as the pure scientist, either. You're too conscious of the individual. Like I am."

"I'm pretty conscious of an individual at the moment," Arch said, coming around the car to open the door for her. The convertible was very low to the ground, and when Susan swung her knees around to alight, she seemed to be miles lower than Arch's tall reach. The distance was a minor detail to Arch.

He leaned toward Susan, put one long arm beneath the bend of her knees, the other around her shoulders.

"You're getting too thin, girl," he told her, holding her close to his chest and talking softly against the pink pearl earring. They were in the shadow of a pine which spread its high branches between them and the stars. Susan leaned her head back against Arch's arm, and saw a streak of light as a star fell.

"I don't feel thin; I feel like I weigh a ton. Put me down, Arch," she said, but her voice was as soft as the night.

"I love you, Susan," Arch said, his voice barely audible above the sound of the wind in the pines. From the beach in front of the Chateau, the surf, too, was muted.

The feel of Arch's mouth when it met Susan's was strong and smooth. The stirring sweetness of that kiss blacked out the night, the falling star, the threatening hulk of St. Patrick's. Even Mavis Pennington.

Then Arch put her down, being sure that her high-heeled pumps were planted firmly on the oyster-shell parking apron. "Come on, Nurse Farley," he said. "I'm starved."

Holding hands, they ran toward the lighted canopy of the Chateau.

CHAPTER XIII

It was Susan's day off.

While she had no money of her own to spend, her happiness over the short telephone conversation she'd had early this morning with Ma Maggie was as complete as if the hundred-dollar bill in her purse were really hers.

Actually, it belonged to Oliver Cox. Immediately on the heels of Mrs. Branch's phone call had come one from the bedside phone in Room 212.

"Could you do some shopping for me, Susan?" the deep voice at the other end of the line inquired.

"Yes, Mr. Cox," Susan said promptly.

"Amy tells me it's your day off. I'm sending over an envelope with some money. And a list of things I'd like to have. Okay?"

"Okay," Susan agreed.

"You sound as if your voice is doing a ballet," the man said surprisingly.

Susan laughed. "Could be," she agreed. "I'm going to report to Surgery tomorrow. Isn't it wonderful?"

"Tomorrow . . ." Cox sounded thoughtful. Susan was conscious of a slight loss of some of her elation. Then she took another look at herself. Why should Oliver Cox care whether she worked in Surgery or not?

I guess I'm getting into the habit of expecting too much from people, Susan thought. Aloud, she assured Oliver Cox that it would be a pleasure to do his errand.

The contents of the envelope, when it came by messenger, astonished Susan.

Fixed to the hundred-dollar bill was a note.

"Dear Susan," the scrawling handwriting said. "Please use this to buy the following: Half a dozen of those scarves to use as a sling; I'm going to get out of here first thing you know, and I won't have any proper badge to show I'm not fit for a good fight, yet.

"And it's going to be cold weather soon; I'd like to buy a red sweater for Pat. Nothing pink or blue. It's gotta be red. And a cap to match.

"Then get something nice for Amy. She'll be going off duty from taking care of me tomorrow, and I'd like her to have something to put her in mind of the bad-tempered labor man from the North—she's got an idea it's some kind of disgrace, nursing a Yankee. If it isn't enough money, call me and I'll send more. Thanks. Oliver."

Susan's step was as light as her heart as she walked past the windows of the more fashionable and expensive Palm City shops.

Accustomed to making most of her own clothes, and getting those she did buy from the big department stores that had come to Palm City as a result of its rapid growth in the last ten years, Susan didn't usually even window-shop here where the customers were almost entirely from the resort hotels. They drove over from the east end of the island, clad in the latest thing in beach wear, and casually picked up little items like cocktail dresses or cashmere sweaters that would cost what Susan made in a month. Occasionally, accident or illness brought some of them to St. Patrick's. Susan and the other nurses found their brief contact with the world of the wealthy interesting and exciting, but they knew that while the patronage of these visitors was helping to make Palm City prosper, their two worlds were as far apart as another planet.

It was because of Amy's wistful admiration of a white cashmere sweater one such patient at the hospital had worn away, draped carelessly over bronzed shoulders, that Susan had come to this glamorous end of Clematis Street.

She had found a parking place between a Cadillac and a Thunderbird, and had carefully maneuvered the old Farley sedan into place at the curb. "Excuse us," Susan mentally addressed the sleek conveyances. Of the two, she thought the fire-engine-red Thunderbird more to her taste. She put a coin in the parking meter, and stood admiring the red leather upholstery.

It gave her something of a jolt when two girls of her own age brushed past her and got into the Thunderbird. One of them was Mavis Pennington. She slid under the wheel of the sports car, her white jersey pleated skirt, with its matching top and red scarf, just the right foil for her pert blonde beauty. With a powerful purr, the captive horsepower came to life under the long hood, and Mavis' hands on the steering wheel—crimson tipped this morning, Susan noted—skillfully extracted the car from its crowded parking space.

She's a bit beyond the scratching-off stage, Susan thought critically, *but as gorgeous a rig as that is bidding for the limelight all the time.*

She watched the red car until it was out of sight. Mavis hadn't seen Susan, she was sure; Dr. Mitchell's niece was headstrong and heedless, but Susan didn't think she was a snob. Her work at the hospital, as an auxiliary, had shown her to be thoughtful of the patients. Susan sighed. Arch had teased her about her jealousy of Mavis.

"She's a good kid," he had said. And Susan had let it go at that. It wasn't too hard to do, after that shared kiss outside the Chateau.

Firmly, Susan went about her business of hunting the right sweater for Amy. It had to be white; Amy would want to wear it on duty, for the air-conditioning made a sweater mandatory, even in the summer months. It couldn't be full of bead trim; that would be inappropriate. Susan wanted it to be of that lovely, velvety kind of yarn that made the knitted garment look almost like chamois. It would take some hunting.

Accustomed as she was to the department-store brand of headlining a sale with banners and bold-face type, it was with considerable amusement that Susan noticed the windows here were labeled with small, dignified signs, in a late-summer effort to turn over their inventories. "Reductions."

At the fourth shop, Susan discovered Amy's sweater, just as she had planned it should look. Its luxurious softness cost enough to make Susan draw in her breath sharply, but she'd made the purchases of Cox's other things first, to allow for this. *The wrapping alone is worth what a sweater usually costs*, Susan thought, putting the package on the front seat beside her.

This had been a nice errand. She'd enjoyed every minute of it. The Sisters at St. Patrick's who had special charge of young Patrick Durrance would be delighted with the red sweater and hat. Amy, with her meticulous way of treating things, would make the fabulous sweater last a lifetime. Susan was taking the parcels, and change of a dollar and nine cents, to the man in Room 212.

Oliver Cox's strong face lighted up when she arrived, shortly after four. He was in the big chair, arrayed once more in the resplendent robe.

"Thought you'd never get here," he greeted her.

"I prolonged it as much as I could—I had such a good time spending someone else's money."

"Put 'em down over there." Cox waved his good hand at the table which served as a bed table for meals. Amy strove valiantly to keep it free of papers and books. "And sit down, for Pete's sake. You make me nervous."

Out of uniform, Susan sat. She sighed deeply, pleasantly tired. "I've got to go home," she said, making no effort to move. "Dinner to fix. Amy would never approve of the way my kitchen looks."

"Will you have dinner with me, Susan?" Oliver Cox said, with no preamble to cushion her surprise.

"What?" Susan opened her blue eyes to their widest.

"Not here. I'm having a few guests at the De Soto." Cox let something of his delight over Susan's astonishment show in the usually unreadable black eyes.

"A celebration?" Susan asked. She wasn't sure she wanted to go. Oliver Cox was a domineering, forceful person. He assumed a brusque leadership over anyone with whom he came into contact. It was as natural to him as breathing.

Susan's chin lifted unconsciously. She liked him as a patient; they'd become friends, after a fashion. But Susan knew the almost unvarying law of life that erased the hospital world from the mind of its inmates once they rejoined the everyday rush of their normal lives.

Oliver Cox was watching the play of Susan's thoughts across her expressive face. She became aware of his searching look, and the quick blush stained her translucent skin. She got up from her chair and walked over to the window, to hide her reaction. But Cox, who had lived long in the area of human reactions, sensed her reluctance. More, he was immediately aware of its cause.

"You don't want any part of me, socially, do you, Susan?" he asked abruptly. He didn't wait for her answer; instead, he swept on, giving his own reasons as far as he cared to do so.

"This isn't any champagne-in-the-bucket kind of a deal I'm asking you to. When I'm ready to invite you for personal reasons, it won't be with a lot of fuddy-duddies who spend their time cutting out the rotten spots in people." Susan turned from her contemplation of the bay and the spreading panorama of Palm City's shoreline. With serious eyes, she listened to Cox. His face, always serious, was somber now, but the black eyes were blazing with anger.

"It's largely on your account I got all these sawbones together. If you don't like 'em, we'll send 'em packing. But I must say I'm disappointed in you, Susan. You've taught me a lot, but I won't stand being patronized, not by you or anyone else."

"Was I patronizing?" How could she *be* such a stuffed shirt! Oliver Cox had shown more greatness of spirit than any man she'd ever known. "Of course I'll come, Oliver." The name came naturally from her lips. She didn't notice it; but Cox's eyes softened.

"Sawbones? This is a dinner for doctors?" Susan asked interestedly. "Are you sure you want me there? I can't see how I could contribute . . ."

"You contributed the idea of the whole thing," Cox said stubbornly. "What's the matter with you, Susan? Don't you *want* to go to a dinner for the famous Hubbard?"

"*Hubbard!*" Susan's eyes shone. "Hubbard's here?" It was like being introduced to Lister, or Ochsner, or Pasteur. Hubbard was one of the pioneers who had proved that cancer in animals was the result of viruses. He was working now on a vaccine to prevent cancer virus. While mice were his subjects, everyone in the medical world knew that men were the ultimate goal. "I can't wait to tell Arch." Susan reached for her purse.

"Doc Curtis knows," Cox said drily. "He's handling the details."

"He didn't tell *me*."

"Professional secret," Cox said, grinning at her feminine reaction. "Besides, this is my show." The black eyes glinted. "Run along, since you must." The thin lips smiled at Susan's obvious urgency to be gone. "And dress up," he called to her as she went out the door.

Susan retraced her flying steps. "Oh, Oliver, I forgot. What time?"

"One of my boys is coming to pick me up," Cox told her. "While I've learned to walk all over again, the hospital folks don't think I'm as well as I know I am. They'll wheel me down to the car. We'll come for you at eight. Okay?" The deep voice held a half-hidden chuckle.

"Okay!" Susan gave a salute, and was gone.

At the elevator, she had a dismaying thought. What would she wear?

It has to be festive, she thought, driving toward home. *It must have dignity—nothing frilly.* She rejected the thought of borrowing Grace's new white organdie. The organdie was a bit on the ingenue side. Definitely not for Dr. Hubbard.

"And not the black sheer." She ruled out her semi-formal, because of its thin straps and bare-shoulder effect.

By the time she got home, she was in despair. It was no use. She'd call up and beg off.

Her sister met her at the door. "Can I have Jimmy to supper?" Grace began. "I've got spaghetti sauce on; it's been simmering for hours. You want to ask Arch? Papa's fine." The younger girl said it all at once, not stopping for comment from Susan. She was immediately aware of Susan's dejection.

"Are you fired again?" Grace was big-eyed with apprehension.

"My goodness, no!" Susan had to laugh. "I'm going to a dinner that's the most important thing that ever happened to me, and I haven't got anything to wear."

"Oh." Grace sat down at the breakfast-alcove table. This was trouble she could understand. Her dark brows met in a frown. "Don't talk. Let me think." She did so, while Susan went in to visit with John Farley.

"What's the commotion?" her father asked with a twinkle. Susan kissed him, thinking that nothing quenched the quiet kindness of those deep-set eyes. She explained her dilemma, making light of it.

"How much time do you have?" he asked.

"Three hours. If it was three weeks, I might be able to whip something together. As it is, I'm temporarily embarrassed." She gave her father the afternoon paper and turned on the reading light by the bed.

"Susan." The quiet command in his voice stopped her at the door.

"Sir?" Susan raised her brows.

"Right now, you are very much like your mother."

"Thanks, darling." The dimple showed briefly.

"I'm not passing out idle compliments. You know, she was exactly your size and coloring when we married. That was in the late twenties, and haven't I heard you and Grace comment on the recessive tendency of female fashions?" John Farley's conversation was often apt to be pedantic. "I was thinking. Susan's wedding dress is on a hanger at the back of my closet, sealed in a brown paper bag. You remember?"

Susan's eyes filled with quick tears. Of course she remembered. The exquisite white transparent velvet, starkly simple in its fashioning. She had seen her mother's slim hands hold it with loving touch, and it was so much a part of the other Susan Farley that since her death it had remained untouched by anyone else.

"It's the right size," Susan said thoughtfully. "I'm sure of that." She walked to the big closet and found the hanger. Her father watched her with inscrutable eyes.

Grace came in then. "What are you two doing, rattling paper in here?" Her brown eyes took in the situation immediately. She sat down abruptly on the bed. "Of course!" she breathed.

With hands that trembled a little, Susan extracted the shimmering loveliness of the gown from its inner covering of muslin.

"It looks like mother-of-pearl," Grace whispered.

"It looks like moonlight on the bay." Susan moved it gently, watching the lamplight catch the silken pile of the velvet, faded now to a soft ivory that enhanced its original beauty.

"It looks like Susan Farley," their father said.

Susan vanished, was gone only seconds, and returned in the dress. Its scalloped hemline reached just below her shapely knees. She looked doubtfully at the length.

"Your mother's legs were better," John Farley said critically.

After a second, he joined in the spontaneous burst of laughter from the two girls, though Susan knew that the catch in her throat must be in his, too. But her mother would like this, she felt.

It was wonderful that fall was so imminent; the velvet was just the right advance on the season; it was light as feathers on a lark's breast. Susan said so.

"A lark." Her father's eyes were fixed on his yesterdays as Susan left the room.

CHAPTER XIV

There was no denying the thrill of being collected in Oliver Cox's long black Cadillac, chauffeured by one of "the boys." And added to this was Cox's obvious enjoyment in being her escort, his open admiration of Susan's appearance—"You should always wear white, even away from the hospital. It makes you glow, sort of shining—and with one of those circlets of light around your head like in church," he told her seriously.

"A halo, Oliver?" Susan laughed, but she was pleased. It must have been the glinting light on the chiffon velvet dress. Susan smoothed it with loving fingers. What slight wrinkles it had acquired, being crowded against the wall in the closet, had shaken free in the steaming humidity of the Farley bathroom.

Oliver Cox was a contradiction himself, in the tailored severity of his dark dinner clothes. The black silk scarf that served as a sling was hardly noticeable. Privately, however, Susan thought the barbaric bathrobe suited him better. There was a pirate-like quality to Oliver Cox.

"Black mustachios and a blade between his teeth," Susan murmured, from her corner. Oliver was talking to the driver. But he heard her.

"You think I'd look all right with a mustache?" he asked. "I never had one. Might do, at that."

"I was just thinking out loud," Susan said. How could she explain? Oliver would never understand the allusion. He'd be hurt, thinking she considered him an outlaw. She didn't. Oliver was a law unto himself.

Oliver rubbed his long upper lip with a speculative finger. "Might do," he repeated.

But the easy, friendly atmosphere was gone. Susan could think of nothing to say. Oliver couldn't, or wouldn't, either. The silence grew.

They were crossing the long causeway, the bay beneath them only hinted at by the occasional shimmering reflection of starlight.

"It's a long way to the District, eh, Ben?" Oliver addressed the driver.

"Yeah. Not just all this water, neither," Ben replied.

"You like Florida, Ben?" Susan asked. "Keep the conversation on the surface," she told herself. Some sixth sense began to suspect that Oliver Cox might will it otherwise.

"I like this part of it. This ain't Florida, not Miami-like," Ben answered.

"Not yet, anyway," Susan agreed. "We're working folks in northwest Florida. Even the people who come here to play are working folks back home, rather than the moneyed visitors on the Gold Coast. It makes a difference."

Oliver Cox said nothing. From the corner of her eye, Susan could see that he was watching her. At any rate, he was turned her way. Ahead of them, the low-lying trees of the Island, the one tall building (their destination), the neon lights and the colored flood lamps of the string of motels on both bayshore and the Gulf—contrasts of color and darkness against the moonless sky—looked like an Aladdin's cave. Susan said so.

"Who was Aladdin?" Oliver Cox's voice was low. It shut Ben out of the conversation.

"A peasant boy who wished for wealth, and found it brought its own troubles."

"You want to tell me about him?" Oliver's deep voice was a contradiction to the small-boy wistfulness it held. Aladdin was a safe topic. In her clear voice, Susan related the story of the genius in the lamp. Ben, too, was listening, she saw. Somewhat carried away by the attention of her listeners, and the beauty of the Island night, Susan improvised. She made Aladdin a sort of swashbuckling fairy godfather, loving children and helping the poor and the sick. Too late, she realized the error of her ways. For when she had finished, when the big Cadillac pulled up before the marquee of the De Soto Hotel, Oliver Cox's strong right hand, with its fingers that had the strength of steel—a working man's fingers that knew the feel of cables and wrenches—found Susan's on the car seat. He held her hand in his for a paralyzing moment, and then, as abruptly, let it go. He got out on the far side of the car, waving away the doorman who would have opened the door for Susan. This job, Oliver Cox did himself.

And he practically has to hold onto the car to get around it, Susan thought, the nurse in her coming to the fore. She had to stifle an impulse to jump out of the car and help him up the curb. *Velvet dress and all,* she thought hysterically. This evening showed signs of getting out of hand.

"Well, Arch will be here," she reassured herself. Arch and Dr. Mitchell had the famous visitor in tow. The other members of St. Patrick's Board would be here, too. "I never *was* so out of place," Susan murmured aloud. As usual, Oliver heard her. *He has the ears of a woods creature,* she thought, realizing that the smile he gave her was meant to be reassuring. *Oh, goodness! With that salt-and-pepper hair sticking up as if it's going to spring out of his scalp with vigor, and those slightly pointed ears—I declare, he really does look like a well-tailored wolf!*

The elevator stopped at the top floor. The dinner was to be in the penthouse dining room. Susan had never been up here before.

The walls were great picture windows, their soft green draperies drawn back to disclose the panorama of coastline and the water world beneath them.

"It's like being on a boat, or in a plane," she exclaimed, walking over to the windows and holding her hands like blinders, shutting out the soft light of the room.

"I thought you'd like it here," the man at her elbow said in that "just-us-two" tone. Susan dropped her hands immediately, and turned back to the room.

The long table in its center was a picture of pale pink damask and pink and gold china. Goblets with golden mermaids twined around them were at each place, matching wineglasses beside them. At spaced intervals were golden bowls of pink snapdragons. Susan leaned against the window sill, watching the other guests come in small groups. She counted nineteen. Arch was last.

Susan was the only woman. Her heart-shaped face flamed with the blush she knew was there. That was when Arch raised his eyebrows as he met her look. Hadn't he expected her to be here?

Suddenly, Susan wished she weren't. But Oliver was bringing Dr. Hubbard over. Susan stood very straight, and the color drained out of her face as suddenly as it had come.

"This is Miss Farley, Doctor," Oliver was saying.

"We are privileged, sir," Susan murmured. She inclined the head whose darkly red waves were in such contrast to the whiteness of her skin and gave him her hand, realizing that her mother's choice of crushed sleeve made a woman's hand, emerging from the wrist-length fabric, seem fragile and feminine. This was the night to have used some of Grace's nail polish, but Susan hadn't thought of it until now. And what a silly thing to pop into a girl's mind, at a moment like this. Her blue eyes shone and the dimple ducked in and out.

Susan, sitting shyly at the far end of the long table, had little to say during the dinner that was a gourmet's dream. All the famous seafood dishes that were native to the Florida panhandle, plus some of Oliver Cox's city preferences. The speeches afterward were mostly about what could be accomplished in a cancer clinic in the Deep South. There were references to the work being done in New Orleans, but, it was remarked, Florida's sunshine had more ultraviolet than Louisiana's, and far more sun bathers. The Cox clinic plan was hailed as big news in the medical world.

When the table introductions were made, Oliver Cox briefly introduced Susan as a nurse with a dream to work in cancer surgery.

Susan, meeting Arch's look across the table, down three or four places, thought he looked perplexed. She tried to telegraph a query, but he looked away; perhaps, she told herself, because the man next to him touched his arm just then.

Dr. Christopher Mitchell sat at the head of the table; Aloysius Duffy at the foot. It was the first time since her graduation that Susan had seen Dr. Mitchell under a good light. The corridors of St. Patrick's weren't too well illuminated; or maybe she just hadn't looked at him. There was a white scar on his handsome nose that she hadn't noticed before. And on the outer rim of the scar, unmistakably a radium burn, was an angry red blotch. Susan's brows met in a quick frown. She wondered if Arch had noticed. Of course he had. It was his business to notice cancer.

"Susan Farley, the famous diagnostician," she scornfully addressed herself. But unbidden, there came to her mind the picture of the terribly disfigured blonde she had seen in Dr. Thomas's office. Susan was sure something could be done about that woman's face; she'd seen Arch work greater magic than that, with his skilled surgeon's fingers and a patch of skin from some part of the patient's body. Arch could make her a new mouth.

But what would Dr. Mitchell do about his nose? Susan withdrew her attention from it; first thing she knew, he would meet her eye, and she didn't want to risk an open snub.

And as much as she was enjoying the talk, Susan was ill

at ease. No one but Oliver Cox, a man who made his own rules, would have invited her here. She was glad when the last polite applause put a period to the last eulogy of the union's generosity. Oliver Cox, Susan thought anxiously, was overplaying his strength. There was a tired droop to his eyelids.

In the confusion of chairs being pushed back, and hands being shaken, Susan made her way to Arch. He was talking in a low voice to Al Duffy. Timidly, Susan touched his arm. He turned, the spark that always flashed between them reassuring her about his feeling for her. It was strange, her need for constant and repeated reassurance from Arch. Why didn't she just accept him, as he apparently did her?

His greeting was a shock to her. "Oh, good evening, Susan. Don't you think your patient is overstaying his strength?" Not a word about how she looked, not a hint of comfort from him for her feeling lost all evening, when she'd been so sure he would understand.

"That's what I came to ask you," Susan said, lifting her chin. "I think he'd go home now if you spoke to him."

"You mean you don't think your influence would reach that far?" Arch's left eyebrow lifted in a look of cynicism.

Susan bit her lip. How dared he? Mr. Duffy certainly had heard . . .

Without a word, she turned and slipped out through the sliding doors, pulling them softly to behind her. With a finger that shook, she pushed the button for the self-service elevator, thankful that there would be no operator to witness her tears. She had no power at all to keep them from spilling over. The handkerchief in her tiny white evening bag proved wholly inadequate.

In the lobby, she went swiftly to a telephone booth. She would phone Grace to come for her. Then she changed her mind. A cab would cost a small fortune, but it would be worth it not to have Dad know what a fiasco her evening had turned out to be. It would break his heart if she hadn't had a wonderful time in the velvet gown. Where, she wondered, was the dollar she kept in her compact for emergencies? It wasn't there now, anyway. All she could find in her purse was a lone dime.

She dialed the taxicab number. It would take awhile, the dispatcher said. She thought quickly. If she waited in front of the hotel, the dinner crowd would be flocking out and she'd be conspicuous.

She told the man to pick her up in front of the florist's

shop around the corner from the main entrance. Then she got paper from the desk, and left a note for Oliver with the doorman.

Susan waited, feeling very small in front of the dark shop windows. Her feet, in their white satin pumps, were beginning to hurt; her anger was diminishing, and she began to worry that maybe the cab wasn't coming after all.

She moved back and forth, not daring to go far for fear the cab would come. Oliver would be fuming, and probably give her a dressing down. Arch wouldn't be thinking of her. He didn't care how she got home, obviously. Firmly she checked the threatening flood of self-pity.

There was no denying the fact that it was getting late. Traffic along the main artery of the Island had slowed to an occasional speeding car.

Well, she might as well face it. The cab had had plenty of time to get here. It wasn't coming. What now?

"Go back into the hotel and ask the desk clerk to call a cab for you, or cash a check. He doesn't know me, and I have no credentials in this excuse for a purse," Susan reasoned. But surely he would telephone for her. She should have done this sooner.

A car slowed as she emerged from the recessed doorway of the florist's shop. A pear-shaped whistle advertised the intent of the car's occupants to offer her a lift. Ignoring them, she raised her chin and walked firmly back around the corner. The doorman who had been there earlier was long since off duty. The lobby lights were dimmed.

Just as Susan turned to re-enter the De Soto's plate-glass doors, there was a flash of red at the curb and a beep from the horn of an expensive low-slung car that pulled to a stop.

"Hi–you're the nurse on Second, East, aren't you?" The young voice that hailed Susan could belong to no one else but Dr. Mitchell's niece. Susan spun around. Mavis Pennington was alone in the fire-engine-red Thunderbird, her dark curls blown riotously free from the speed she'd been driving.

Susan wouldn't have believed she could be so glad to see Mavis.

"Could you–would you give me a lift home?" Susan walked over to the side of the low car.

"That's a doll dress you have on . . . What's your name? Mine's Mavis."

"Susan Farley. Would you mind?"

"Of course not. Good thing you had on a white dress. I always see Girls in White. Always wanted to be a nurse, myself. Uncle said no. Not smart enough, I guess, though he tried to make it sound as if his sister's daughter shouldn't work for a living. So I'm a Girl in Pink, see?"

Susan, sitting low in the seat beside the beautiful girl at the wheel, saw that she was, indeed, a Girl in Pink. The cotton knitted dress seemed to be almost sprayed on the lovely figure.

The powerful motor under the long hood roared, and the car sprang forward. Mavis' dainty foot in its pointed pink slipper pushed down on the accelerator. There was no one else on the road; on two wheels the Thunderbird made the right-angle turn of the approach to the causeway.

"Must we go so fast?" Susan was genuinely frightened. She hated to remonstrate with the girl at the wheel. Particularly so, after her glimpse into the unhappiness behind the cameo-like beauty.

"Want to show you how fast she'll go," Mavis screamed into the wind that tore at their faces. Susan's feet were pressed tightly to the floorboards.

A late-comer to the beaches drove toward them on the causeway approach. Mavis must either have been blinded by the lights or misjudged her place on the fill. The red car careened farther to the right than the roadbed extended. Speeding tires found no traction in the soft sands of the shoulder.

Susan heard herself praying aloud. The rocks that formed a shallow jetty of protection when tides were high seemed to rush toward them. Then the car turned crazily. The dome of the night sky was sideways; then it was lost.

Susan felt herself flung free of the somersaulting automobile. Shallow backwater broke her fall. She lay there, feeling the cool wet sand against her back and legs and head. With great gasping gulps, she tried to draw breath into her lungs.

Then she got painfully to her knees, and crawled to the overturned car.

"Mavis?" she called, not recognizing the hoarse voice that was hers. "Oh, dear Lord, make her safe."

An outflung hand, the slender fingers curved in a sort of beckoning way, showed their pink lacquered polish in the headlights of the other car that had stopped and turned, and parked. Men came sliding, slipping, shouting down the embankment. Susan's nurse's hands searched the body of the other girl for broken bones. There were lacerations, for there was blood matting the dark curls. Susan saw the red stain on the white velvet dress. "Find the pressure point," her nurse's mind telegraphed.

Until the ambulance came, she sat in the sand and kept her fingers firmly pressed against the throbbing artery under the curls against the almost frail temple.

Susan rode in the ambulance with Mavis. She held the girl's cold hand when the litter bearers carefully transferred the slight body to the waiting guerney at the door of Emergency. And not once did she release her pressure on the scalp artery.

She stood, her teeth chattering with reaction, waiting for the resident to come with his merciful hypodermic.

It would be Arch, she was sure.

"Susan?" She heard his voice from a long way off.

Then she let go of Mavis' small hand, and slipped to the floor.

CHAPTER XV

It was Grace who handed Susan a cup of hot tea to drink when she awoke.

"For a girl who has always been on the quiet side, you manage to crash the headlines more than anyone I ever heard of," her sister told her.

"I've got the grandfather of all headaches." Susan put both hands to her head. They told her that her hair was braided as she always did it at bedtime. She realized then that she was at home; that the sunlight against the shades denoted the day to be well advanced.

"No wonder," Grace commented.

Memory of the wreck flooded back into Susan's mind with all the impact of a ballistic missile. "Mavis?" She sat up in bed.

"She's going to pull through, they think, thanks to your being there to stop the flow of blood. Dr. Mitchell wanted you to have what corresponds to the bridal suite at the hospital, but Dad thought you'd rather be home, since sleep and rest were all you need." Grace was moving around, putting the room to rights.

Susan's white satin pumps were in the middle of the floor, a sorry sight, with mud encrusted all over them. Her hose were shreds of wispy nylon, half in and half out of the wastebasket. Grace had the velvet dress in her hands when Susan put down her teacup.

"I didn't do this sooner, for fear of disturbing you," Grace explained. "Besides, I thought if I took them out before, Dad would see all this . . ." Her voice trailed off into silence.

The two girls looked at the dress they had thought was moonlight and starshine. It was hopelessly ruined. The browning reddish blotches, half covering the front, where Susan had held Mavis' head close, would never come out; the back was sand and mud.

"Did he see me come in with that on?" Susan swallowed painfully.

"No. Dr. Mitchell sent you in the ambulance that was already there, and there was a sheet over you. What in the world were you doing with Mavis Pennington?" Grace had put the ruined clothes in a brown paper bag and hidden it under a beach towel. She sat down now at the foot of Susan's bed.

Susan took a shaken breath. Grace had a right to know. She gave an account of the evening's happenings.

"Why did you leave without Mr. Cox?" Grace asked bluntly.

"I thought he'd want to visit around with the men, and I could pick up a cab," Susan said.

"And why didn't you?"

"It never came," Susan explained. "I thought I had a dollar bill tucked inside my compact; I always do. It seems incredible that the mere lack of change in a person's purse could result in all this."

"I got the dollar, one day last week," Grace confessed. "The paper boy came to collect, and there wasn't any money in the house. I remembered you always kept that dollar in your compact, so I borrowed it, intending to pay it back from the house budget."

Susan was ready to get up. She swung her legs around and put her slim feet into mules. "I'd better call Mrs. Branch and find out whether I have a job or not," she said. "And I want to see Mavis, poor little thing– You know she wants to be a nurse?"

"Dr. Mitchell said for you to rest and not worry," Grace said.

"I'll surely worry if I rest," Susan commented, getting her clothes together. Her alarm clock showed it to be nearly noon. "What are you doing home from class?"

"Well, I had a light schedule today, and I wanted to be sure you were all right." Grace disclaimed any feeling over Susan's escape, but her brown eyes showed traces of tears, and there were dark circles under them.

"What's Dad doing?" Susan straightened the seams of her hose.

Grace grinned. "Fixing you some lunch."

"Oh, no!" Susan groaned. Their father's single culinary accomplishment was a concoction he called chili, but both girls thought no self-respecting Mexican would touch the stuff.

"He thinks you need something real tasty," Grace explained.

"I could maybe, just maybe, stand a soft-boiled egg," Susan said.

"With tamales, out of a can," Grace elaborated.

Both girls laughed, but it was an indulgent sort of laughter, filled with the pleasure of knowing their father had come sufficiently along the road to recovery to move around the house.

"Has Arch called?" Susan asked casually buttoning her uniform down the front. Her shoes could stand a real polishing, but a swipe or two with a whitened sponge would have to do.

"Well, it's only noon," Grace answered. "But Mr. Cox called. He wants you to come by his room before you get involved with duty."

Susan was ready. The demands of regular duty, any kind of regular duty, would be the only escape for her from this underlying sense of uneasiness. She was willing to let more competent minds than hers worry about the cancer clinic, about what would become of young Durrance, about whether or not the woman in Dr. Thomas' office ever got her lip resurfaced.

I must be getting some kind of sense knocked into my head, she thought. The feeling stayed with her, making it possible for her to appear to enjoy the steaming bowl of garlic-scented chili her father had deposited before them.

"Nothing like some good, tangy tomato taste to give you a zestful feeling," he had told them.

"Ninety-eight degrees, the weather man said today," Grace remarked innocently. "A person really needs all the zest possible."

Susan dropped her sister off at the campus. "You be careful," Grace told her. "I never know, when I leave you, what will happen to you before I see you again."

"Stop clucking," Susan told her sister. But it was the first time in years—in their lives, perhaps—that there had been this warmth between them.

Maybe it's been my fault, Susan thought, as a traffic light slowed her. *I always thought Grace was self-centered and that she and Dad were a closed corporation against me.* It was a shattering thought, this new self-evaluation Susan was giving herself.

I might as well relate it to my work, too. She turned the spotlight of her own criticism to her pride in her profession. *I've had the attitude, all along, that St. Patrick's was mighty lucky to have a chance at the services of the dedicated Susan Farley, R.N.*

Susan's face burned. She had wanted more than anything

in the world, to be able to work in Surgery with Arch on his cancer operations, of which he was having more and more, thanks to Dr. Mitchell's tendency to put more time into his office practice.

She couldn't find a parking place, even in the section reserved for House Staff. She put the sedan under an oak tree a block away from the hospital parking lot.

It was this happenstance that made her take the shortcut through the landscaped grounds of the student nurses' dormitory. A white-capped nurse was sitting on the grass in the shade of an oleander bush, watching a baby make swimming-like motions on a beach towel in the sun.

Susan stopped. The baby was Patrick Durrance. He'd grown even in the short time since Susan had seen him last. He was becoming more of an individual, less the typical infant with round head and eyes that were usually apt to be closed in profound sleep that no amount of handling could interrupt.

"Hi, Pat." Susan knelt on one knee and gave her hand to the boy. He took it promptly, making a strong effort to pull Susan nearer.

"We've been out here ten minutes," the nurse said. "Fifteen is as much as His Nibs here is allowed at one time. I've got an errand to do in the dorm; could you stay those five minutes with Pat, Farley? I'll be right back." She was on her feet, taking Susan's acceptance for granted. Everyone jumped at the chance to be with the "hospital's baby." The nurses were spoiling him, Susan had heard. But young Pat Durrance neither knew nor cared.

His great blue eyes regarded Susan with complacent male acceptance of feminine subjugation. Susan sat down beside him.

The lawn was newly mowed. The smell of cut grass in the summer sun was delightful; Susan told him so. "You smell good, too," she assured him, when he put his hand against her cheek, leaving a wet spot and a whiff of baby powder.

"Rullff," Patrick Durrance complimented her in return, falling immediately flat on his full-cheeked face.

Susan scooped him up, which seemed to amuse him enormously.

"I could eat you with a spoon," she said. "But I have to be going, fella; your Registered Sitter had better come back." She looked with some anxiety around the oleander bush. The baby's nurse was coming. Susan got up, brushed off the cut blades of grass from her dress, and rejected the girl's thanks. "We should charge admission to that one," Susan said. "The hospital's financial troubles, if any, after the appearance of our fairy godfather, would be no more."

Susan thought the girl looked at her queerly. But she was late, if she expected to be put on the three o'clock shift.

She had dreaded the interview with Mrs. Branch, remembering the last one. *If Ma Maggie is chilly this time*, Susan thought, with her new-found humility, *I'll try to tell her that I'm sorry for bumbling the hospital into the papers all the time. I bet today's headlines are the worst yet.* But she wasn't going to look at them.

Ma Maggie got up from behind her neat desk and rustled around to greet Susan. "We've been phoning your house," she said crossly. "Where in the world have you been? You're due in Surgery right away. Dr. Mitchell and Dr. Curtis are operating at three-thirty. You'll have to hurry."

Susan didn't stop to ponder on the unpredictability of fate, or make any comment on the Nursing Director's change of front. She was too glad to have it work out this way.

Even if Arch ignored her, she would know the joy of watching his knowing fingers in their superb craftsmanship. For a moment, she knew a stir of curiosity about what sort of case it would be, for Dr. Mitchell to be collaborating; or Arch, she corrected herself. It was difficult for her to subordinate Arch to the Chief of Staff; she considered him by far the superior surgeon.

Susan got off the elevator on the fourth floor and all but ran toward the big double doors extending across the corridor.

She gave no thought to Oliver Cox's message to stop by his room; in the background of her mind, however, was the intention of going by to see how Mavis was getting along. She had intended to offer to do special nursing for the girl, if she were needed. But the call to Surgery made all other matters of secondary importance.

"What gives?" Susan asked the Recovery Room nurse, as she went about the familiar task of preparing herself.

"You mean you don't know?" There was doubt and a hint of jealousy on the girl's face. "This is the famous Mr. Cox's friend from Washington. I understand Dr. Chris has given him the most thorough physical St. Patrick's can dish out. And rumor has it that the poor guy is petrified with fear. He didn't want to go through with it," she added, "but your friend in two-twelve said the word, and here he is."

Susan reverted to her old custom of speaking her mind. "Why *my* friend in two-twelve, Sally?" she asked directly.

Sally's eyes dropped. She shrugged. And Susan let it go.

Holding her hands upright from the elbow, she shouldered her way into the largest operating room on this floor, the one most often used by Dr. Mitchell.

Two doctors whom Susan knew to be Palm City's most sought-after anesthesiologists stood readying the gas tube. Although the big lights over the table were on, the patient was not yet here.

Arch and Christopher Mitchell and another man in gown, cap, and mask were peering at an X-ray mounted on a screen behind which a powerful light burned—the alimentary canal of the patient, showing all the vital organs in perfect relief.

Dr. Mitchell, a scalpel in his gloved hand, made sketching motions at a cloudy spot on the photograph. "Here," he said clearly from behind his mask, "and here. Shouldn't take too long."

"You can never say ahead of time," the stranger commented, turning to check the cart bearing the scalpels, scissors, artery forceps, and needle holders. Susan knew a moment of pride in the fact that the equipment of St. Patrick's was as modern as money could buy. Her blue look flashed around the wall, at the sterile cases holding the self-retaining retractors, the electrically motivated instruments, the instruments tipped with lights to illuminate body recesses, and the all-important oxygen gear.

Her searching gaze met the eye of the head nurse, and she knew an added feeling of satisfaction. There was no one under whom she'd rather work than Leslie O'Neill. The warm eyes smiled, above the green mask, and O'Neill's acknowledgment of Susan's signaled greeting made her feel genuinely happy for the first time that day.

Then the patient was wheeled in. O'Neill beckoned Susan over to the guerney.

"He was held in number two until the Demerol and atropine capsule took hold," she whispered. "Doc Curtis didn't want the poor man to be too frightened. He resisted the sedation like a tiger."

"What will they administer?" Susan whispered back. She wanted to know every detail.

Leslie O'Neill was adjusting the blood-pressure cuff on the patient, the doctors still in their pre-operative huddle. "An injection of sodium pentathol; he'll be under in ten seconds."

The anesthesiologist was suiting his action to her words. He fitted the cone over the patient's face, and Susan saw that they were going to administer cyclopropane gas.

All of Susan that wasn't a trained nurse drained out of her now.

Across the operating table, she met Arch's brown eyes fleetingly. She felt the same electric response, but it only served to accentuate what she gave of herself to her work. The stranger had the scalpel, now, and was talking as he worked.

"There's a measure of rigidity where the former incision was made; adhesions, no doubt," he commented. Susan, with a shock, realized that she was assisting at an operation being conducted by the great Dr. Hubbard.

Arch, and even Christopher Mitchell, moved only at the specialist's bidding. All three men worked swiftly, and with the kind of decisiveness in their movements that bespoke their sureness and knowledge.

When the muscular innerlining was pierced, and the abdomen exposed, the carcinoma's presence in the large intestine was immediately apparent. Arch was reporting on the pulse of the patient; Susan supplied the requested instruments with a dexterity that was second nature to her. Mitchell was placing clamps to keep the cavity from filling with blood.

In what seemed seconds to Susan, the ugly cell mass was excised from its strangle hold, the diseased area cut away, and the first stage was over.

In another ten days, the two ends of the bowel would be sewed together and returned to the abdominal cavity. While it would be five years before he could be sure, at the end of that time, Barney Hopkins would be a free man again.

At the thought of Oliver Cox, Susan thought of her promise to look after the patient's wife—Alice, Oliver had said.

She looked over to where Arch had been, but he had gone.

She was spared the necessity of explaining to him that she'd promised Oliver to look after Mrs. Hopkins. Unreasonably, she knew a return of the heartache that Arch's attitude about Cox had caused.

It slowed her steps as she started for Second, East. Mrs. Hopkins, she was sure, would be waiting with Oliver.

CHAPTER XVI

Alice Hopkins, a pale, timid-looking woman with red-rimmed eyes, was sitting bolt upright in a straight chair. Susan's heart wept for her. From her own experience, she knew that waiting for news like this was a sort of crucifixion.

"He's in the recovery room, now," she told Mrs. Hopkins before Oliver Cox could make the introduction. "The operation was a success, and I can tell you that case histories of this kind of surgery are most encouraging."

Tears welled up into the gray eyes that seemed to be put in with a smutty finger, so deep were the dark circles around them. Alice Hopkins drew a breath that was a long, broken sigh.

"I told her she had the best help there was." Oliver Cox spoke for the first time. "I knew you'd be along. That is," he made his voice colorless, "if you got around to it."

Susan's eyebrows flew up. Oliver, too? Had she no friends at all who weren't put out with her? Her self-condemnatory mood of earlier in the day had worn itself out in the demanding work of the operating room. She looked at him for a steady moment, and decided to say nothing. She was tired from the bottoms of her feet to the top of her head. Thoughts of home and a hot soaking bath, with the prospects of bed immediately after, invaded her mind. Then a look at the forlorn creature in the straight chair made her sigh.

"Have you had dinner, Mrs. Hopkins?" Susan asked gently. "Wouldn't you like me to take you down to the cafeteria, and we can visit while you eat? Your husband will be down from surgery shortly . . . Where will he be?" Susan turned her blue eyes on Cox.

"They moved the boy with the television in two-fourteen," Cox said, a steely glint of humor showing in the black eyes. "I thought he might enjoy that larger room at the other end of the corridor; he seemed very grateful."

Susan smiled. In spite of his moods, she liked Oliver Cox. There was an under-the-surface fire to him. Even when his voice and face were the coldest, flames licked out from those unpredictable caverns that were his eyes. All remoteness fell away from him at her smile.

"Did someone hurt your feelings last night? I thought of every possible explanation of your walking out on me without a word, and that's the only answer I could come up with. Did *I*, for instance?" The look he gave her was pleading.

Alice Hopkins unwittingly came to Susan's rescue. She had been powdering her face, her efforts to cover up the traces of tears making a frightful blotch of her appearance. "I'm ready," she said now. "I look awful, but I couldn't care less."

Susan wanted badly to blurt out to Cox the whole wretched story of her evening. He had meant to be so kind, including her. No, Oliver hadn't offended her. But she wasn't going out with him again; she valued his friendship too much to have a personal element injected into it. She frowned at what he said about her not leaving word. Surely he'd gotten her note? But she'd see him later; she didn't want to go into it now, with Mrs. Hopkins here. So she murmured something about appreciating his kindness, and went out without seeing the stricken look on his strong face.

"I know you'll want to stay with your husband tonight," Susan said, as she and Alice Hopkins waited together for the elevator. "After awhile, perhaps you'll want me to get you a room near the hospital. There are several good places, families who rent rooms to hospital visitors." The car stopped, and they got on. Dr. Mitchell was in the elevator, on his way down from Surgery. He was immaculate in a dark business suit, his black and white mesh oxfords pointing up the almost invisible white stripe in the lightweight summer clothes.

"I want to thank you, myself," he said simply, when Susan got on, followed by Mrs. Hopkins. He didn't think, at first, that they were together. "Mavis is like a spring breeze in my house. It would be grim without her."

"How is she, Doctor?" Susan put her hand on Alice Hopkins' arm, to include her. "I wasn't going to barge in, when she's too ill to see anyone; but if she needs a special—?"

"That's good of you. Particularly good." Susan thought there were more gray hairs at the black temples than there had been in the spring. And that place on the aristocratic nose—her brows met in a frown. Had he seen someone about it? Or was he diagnosing himself?

"I'll remember, in case she does," Dr. Mitchell said, the

dark eyes that had once been so angry warm and responsive now.

"This is Mrs. Hopkins," Susan told him, as they got off in the first floor. "You've met?"

Dr. Mitchell passed his right hand over his eyes and shook his head apologetically. Susan noticed the cut was healed. She felt the blood rush to her face, remembering.

Alice Hopkins, her hand at her throat in a gesture of complete dependence, waited for the surgeon to reassure her about her husband. Dr. Mitchell was kindness itself, explaining that the operation was one that he'd done often, successfully and routinely. "If so serious a thing is ever routine," he added. "I was coming to see you, later."

Susan began to realize why the Chief of Staff had so large a practice. Alice Hopkins was a different person after she'd talked to him. She ate her dinner and paid her check, leaving Susan still eating. Her apology was nonetheless genuine for being slightly breathless. Susan watched her go, a too-thin woman in a dress that didn't fit. But obviously loving, and beloved. And pathetically grateful to Oliver Cox.

Arch came loping in while Susan was having her coffee. He picked up a tray, walked absent-mindedly past the food displayed along the counter, picked up a piece of pie and a dish of red and green gelatin cubes, and a cup of coffee. He brought it over to Susan's table and unloaded the tray, putting the tray in the empty chair so that no one would interrupt them.

"The thing I've always admired most about you," he told Susan, putting sugar into his coffee from the glass container, "was your direct approach. No coy contradictions about Susan Farley. Not my girl. No, sir," he said.

"Your coffee is being invaded," Susan said mildly. "I've doubted lately that single-mindedness is entirely a virtue," she commented.

"That's what I mean," Arch countered, misunderstanding. "If you've got a yen for Oliver Cox, why haven't you told me?"

Susan's jaw dropped. When she got her breath back, she bit her lip in annoyance. Arch Curtis had given her a bad time last night, and he himself had brushed off her mild protest over his taking Mavis around to dances and wherever. And now anything so unreasonable! Susan's eyes flashed blue fire.

"You haven't been around much for me to tell you anything," she said.

"I've been busy—you know that," he growled, stirring the revolting syrup he'd made out of his coffee. "If this cancer clinic doesn't go through, I'm going into private practice. Mitchell has been after me, too."

Susan looked critically at what he'd chosen to eat. "You could do worse," she told him. She got up and went over to the counter, asked for and got a hamburger, complete with sliced tomato and onion, the way she knew he enjoyed it. She marched back to the table and plopped it down before him, moving the pie out of reach. Neither commented on the exchange; Arch picked up the big bun and sank his teeth into it.

When he could, he replied to her comment. "You're kidding."

"No. I've just been thinking, trying to see further than the end of my nose. It seems to me we've both been pretty smug. A man doesn't build up that large a practice without doing a lot of good to a lot of people. Of course he's bound to make mistakes. Everyone does. But if he charges fat fees to people who enjoy poor health, who go to a doctor to dramatize themselves, I'm willing to bet he does plenty of work for which he never gets paid. And did that blonde woman with the bad lip ever go back and *ask* for it to be fixed?" Susan's blue eyes were indignant. She spoke in a rush of low-toned anger.

Arch ate his hamburger, got pretty well through the pie, before he answered her.

"I fixed that woman's lip myself," he said.

Susan's face lighted up. "You *did?* Oh, Arch, why didn't you tell me?"

"Well . . . I haven't had much chance. I called Dr. Thomas right after you told me about her. He sent her around, and I did a lip-resurfacing job. Came out all right, too. Bonnie—her name's Bonnie—says she's going to get her husband back." His brown eyes crinkled and the smile in them spread to his mouth. "Dr. Chris took an afternoon off to play golf with the bank fellow who was the husband's boss. Going to hire him back. Lot of work to being a good doctor." Arch grinned at Susan's obvious happiness over his news. Then his face shadowed again.

"What about Cox?" he asked, pushing the plates out of his way. He put his long arms on the table, crossed them, and looked deep into Susan's eyes.

"What about him?" Susan asked, feeling the pulse in her lower lip begin to tremble. "What about Mavis, since we're being so direct? Poor little thing." Susan was seeing the dark cap of curls against her own white velvet dress, the wheels of the overturned Thunderbird spinning in the air. It was a nightmare, an unforgettable nightmare. She covered her face with her hands.

Arch took them down, not caring who watched. He looked at the neatly cut nails, innocent of lacquer. "Those hands are the hands of a darned good trained nurse. They did a job today, and Hubbard noticed it. Yeah, poor, misdirected little Mavis. I had it out with Dr. Chris. She's going into training in September."

Susan's eyes shone. "Oh, wonderful! Does she know?"

"Yes. He told her this afternoon."

Susan told him about what Mavis had said about her white dress, and the Pink Pinafore. Arch's sensitive face winced. Then warmed, looking at Susan's. Susan felt the slow flush mounting at the way he was looking at her. Suddenly, she felt shy.

"You think I should accept Dr. Chris's bid?" Arch sought safer ground.

"You're the one to decide that," Susan told him with a return of her old directness. "I only said there was something worth considering. But if you do take it," her eyes twinkled, "I advise you to stick it out, because he doesn't like people who change their minds."

"I know what you mean." Arch laughed, then sobered. "Oh. I meant to tell you right off. There's a fine to-do about little Pat Durrance."

"Why?" Susan's heart leaped into her throat. She had learned to love that baby. Somehow, she felt she had a vested interest. Was the baby sick? Not the "hospital's baby."

"The Welfare people told Himself, this afternoon, that it wouldn't allow the hospital to raise Pat. Not for a new cancer clinic, not for all the gold in China. What next, from the unpredictable Mr. Cox?"

Susan sat and stared, her lower lip between her teeth. This was disaster. That baby had become the center of all their dreams. And now they would lose him.

CHAPTER XVII

Susan couldn't call it a day until she had fulfilled her promise to herself to stop in to see Mavis Pennington.

Even after all she'd been through, the girl with the features of a figurine looked lovely when Susan saw her lying against the flat mattress. The pillows that would have pressed against her head wounds were stacked on a nearby chair. At first, Susan thought Mavis was asleep.

But with languid slowness, she opened her eyes.

"Hi." Susan stood near the door, waiting to be sure of her welcome.

"I've been waiting for you to come," Mavis said.

Susan walked over to the bed.

The other girl closed her eyes again. Susan, wise in the ways of shock patients, sat down and waited for the next interval of energy. It came shortly.

"I'm going to enter training in September," Mavis said.

"I'm so glad," Susan said simply.

"Archibald Curtis is in love with you." The dark eyes opened and the beautiful lips smiled slightly.

Susan was startled in spite of herself. Nothing like a brush with death, particularly sudden and violent death, to lessen inhibitions, she thought.

What could she answer? Not knowing whether Mavis was in love with Arch, she certainly couldn't say, "Yes, I believe he is," and anyway, that would sound impossibly smug. So instead, following her newly won knowledge that when in doubt saying nothing was the best rule, she merely patted the small hand that rested limply on the coverlet.

"You're giving him a bad time," was the next revelation from Mavis. She didn't bother to open her eyes to impart this one.

"I haven't meant to," Susan said gently. More than anything, she wanted to ask how. But she feared to excite the patient.

"Did you come to stay with me tonight?" Mavis looked full at Susan, this time. Quick tears filled her eyes.

"If you want me to," Susan promised. She'd have to telephone home. In spite of herself, she sighed with weariness, looking with dislike at the plastic chair.

"Not if you don't want to," Mavis whispered. The tears rolled sideways out of the brown eyes, and slipped unheeded to the pillow.

"Of course I want to. This time yesterday I got myself into a box, and you helped get me out—or you were willing to, anyway," Susan amended hastily. "I hope we can be friends, Mavis," she added. "I've been so wrapped up in learning to be a nurse that I've made fewer real friends among the girls I trained with than almost anyone in the class." Susan put genuine feeling into her bid for the other girl's friendship. It was true. She could use a good friend. And she liked Mavis Pennington.

The hand nearest her, the right hand, came up to hers. Solemnly, the two girls shook hands.

Susan thought Mavis' hand felt hot and dry. When she could do so without being obvious, she went for a thermometer. The mercury showed a degree and a half.

Susan charted it, and reported to the Floor Supervisor that the patient had requested her to remain for the night. She asked about aspirin, and the floor nurse agreed; Susan put two of the white pellets into a crystal container, got a tray, and went back to the room. Mavis had been put on the fifth floor in the only private room available. It was, Susan realized, the only one in the hospital without a view of the bay.

When Mavis was asleep, Susan got up and went to the window overlooking the sprawling city, spread out as far north as she could see.

It was late; the moon was halfway to the zenith in the southeastern sky. Below her, the housetops made a pattern of checkerboard squares, the lighted streets the lines of demarcation.

The town has outgrown us all, Susan thought, noting the unceasing flow of traffic along the highway. *St Patrick's never has any vacant beds, any more, and half the time we have to double up*. Her mind turned to the cancer clinic. It would bring its own problems of housing, for staff and patients. *And the visitors*, she thought, Alice Hopkins in her mind. Three floors down and across the court that formed the space between this wing and Second, East, Alice Hopkins was keeping her night vigil.

Who but Oliver Cox could get a surgical patient into

orthopedics? Susan mused. He seemed to dominate every life that came into contact with his.

Look what he's done to all of us, just knowing him. Susan looked across the court to where in the floodlights St. Patrick kept his vigil. *It's like what our math instructor called the irresistible force and the immovable object. Something happens that isn't always in the books.*

Susan and Arch had speculated on what would happen to Oliver's cancer-clinic plans, in view of the Welfare Board's decision to take over the disposal of the life and affairs of young Pat Durrance.

Arch thought the hospital wouldn't take it to court. "They've always taken the position that foundlings should be handled through channels," he had said. "I don't see how they can reverse themselves without seeming self-seeking. It would be an unhealthy position for an institution, itself a member of the local organization of community services. Himself is fit for psychiatric treatment, he says."

Susan had asked whether Dr. Mitchell had proposed a way out of the impasse.

"He said," Arch replied thoughtfully, "that since the need had been established, as a result of Cox's stirring the thing up, money will likely be made available. Hubbard's being here while all this has boiled over is another factor in our favor. Himself seemed willing for me to go along with things as they are until we know." He was referring to his decision about residency versus private practice.

"I know this much," Susan had concluded. "Whether it is in cancer surgery, general surgery, orthopedics or private duty, even the office duty that I was so horsy about, I'll never again act like a prima donna—not so long as I'm privileged to nurse."

She turned away from her survey of the sleeping city toward the girl in the hospital bed.

Mavis' dark eyes were open. In the dimness of the night light, Susan thought she looked less feverish.

"Hi," she said shyly.

"How do you feel, friend?" Susan smiled over her own choice of the old-fashioned word. Mavis smiled back.

"Better. But my mouth feels like a piece of dry blotting paper."

"How about some hot tea?" Susan offered her own panacea. "I can brew us both a cup."

"Wonderful." Mavis looked pleased. Susan went on quiet

feet to the hall kitchen. She made her own cup quite strong. The night was hardly more than half over.

"Turn up the light, will you, Susan?" Mavis asked when the steaming tea was on her bedside stand.

Susan touched the switch. Mavis said, "I'd like a mirror."

"There isn't any," Susan told her. "Except the dresser over there, and it's out of range."

"You can roll the bed into range, can't you?"

Susan put her strong shoulder against the head of the bed and shoved. Mavis sat up, using her hands as a prop behind her. She made a grimace at what she saw.

"It'll grow back soon," Susan comforted her.

"In plenty of time for me to wear one of those sassy little caps like yours," Mavis said cheerfully.

Susan looked at her with admiration. "You'll do just that," she agreed.

"Now you get a little rest. I'm a selfish pig, or I'd send you home now," Mavis said.

Susan dimmed the lights, and Mavis eased her head back on the pillow. From there, she spoke again.

"I'm terribly sorry I put you through that awful experience. One thing's for sure: I'll never, never exceed the legal speed limit again. In fact," there was a faint chuckle from the bed, "Uncle Chris has grounded me."

"All's well," Susan assured her sleepily. She all but propped her eyes open until she was sure Mavis was sleeping. Then she permitted herself an occasional doze.

But the long night was full of time for thought, and Susan wasn't sorry when the pre-dawn clatter of kitchen activity, audible at this end of the hospital, began.

Mavis woke up at six, demanding coffee. Susan knew the big percolator on Second, East, would be in service by now. It would provide the quickest, best brew. She plumped up Mavis' pillows and fitted them to the patient's back, carefully bypassing the bandaged area.

The coffee was made, filling the floor kitchen with its aroma.

Susan drank her own, and borrowed one of the porcelain cups for Mavis. She was reproaching herself for not learning about cream and sugar, accepting the help of a new nurse's aide whom she didn't know, putting the accessories on a tray. "All this would have been unnecessary if I hadn't been in such a hurry for my coffee," Susan told her. "Oliver Cox has spoiled us all."

"So he has," a deep voice from the doorway commented,

and Susan nearly dropped the tray. She'd completely forgotten that the patient in Room 212 was more than ambulatory now. "Is there enough for me to be spoiled, too?" he asked, leaning with his good elbow against the desk just outside the door.

The aide broke a cup in her confused haste to wait on the man whom everyone in the hospital was talking about. "Here, let me," he offered courteously, stooping to pick up the broken china. It was one of the set he'd bought.

Susan started out, bearing Mavis' tray.

Oliver Cox tightened the belt of his spectacular bathrobe. Satin pajama legs extended below its hem, and matching slippers were on his feet. The scent of his shaving lotion spoke of his early waking. "Can't you stay a moment? I can have my cup here. Okay?" He raised his beetling brows for permission from the aide.

Thoroughly frightened, she gulped and scurried off.

Oliver put a strong hand, whiter than it had probably been since infancy, on Susan's arm. "You won't come to the mountain," he told her lightly, "so I can't let this opportunity go by."

"I've got a patient," Susan said with unintentional primness. When the Floor Supervisor came back to the desk, it would look most unorthodox for Susan to be here, complete with coffee tray going to another floor, and the hospital's most distinguished patient. Particularly, since his attentiveness to her must be common talk by now.

Oliver Cox immediately withdrew his hand. "Don't let me detain you, then," he said.

"Oh, Oliver, don't be difficult . . ."

Cox's stern mouth relaxed and his somber eyes lighted. "Look who's talking," he murmured. But he moved back out of her path. "You *will* stop by before you go home?" he said with an obvious effort to be casual.

Susan agreed. But it was seven-thirty before she had Mavis bathed and freshly gowned. In blue. When Susan had extracted a lovely pink garment from the little suitcase in the closet, Mavis had shuddered. "Not *pink!*" she exclaimed. Both girls laughed in sympathy, and Susan put it back, taking the blue one, instead.

She handed Mavis a book, put the call-light cord where it would be accessible, and on impulse, leaned over and kissed the smaller girl on the cheek.

"This has been good," Susan said simply, "this night together. Thanks for telling me about Arch. I couldn't bear to think of any life that didn't have him in it." Then, without waiting for a reply, she straightened and went out.

She was almost walking in her sleep, but she stopped the elevator at the second floor and took her familiar way around to Room 212.

Mrs. Freeman was briefing the seven-to-three shift when Susan came around the bend in the corridor. She smiled as Susan went by, and Susan waved, pointing to Oliver's room inquiringly. Mrs. Freeman nodded, not stopping her instructions to the oncoming shift. But Susan's heart expanded almost to the bursting point. For whatever reason, she was grateful for the wave of good-will that followed in her wake. "I work like crazy trying to make everyone like me, and what do I get? A deep freeze. Then I nearly get killed in an automobile wreck, after behaving like a spoiled child, instead of facing up to my obligations as a guest, and what happens? Everyone smiles." Susan put both hands in her pockets and lifted her shoulders. It was a crazy world. But a good one.

Then she was knocking on the door of Room 212.

"Come in!" the deep voice responded.

Oliver Cox was dressed in slacks and sports shirt, his still badly swollen hand resting in one of the black silk scarves she'd bought for him.

"You look beautiful!" Susan teased. Oliver beamed.

"You, too, like always," he countered. Susan felt herself blush. She'd practically asked for that one.

"Sit down, Susan." Oliver pointed to the big chair. "And don't mention those corny rules," he said with vehemence. "I've got no time for rules."

Susan sat, but uneasily. Oliver's hand gave her shoulder a push, to settle her against the back.

"I'm being fired out of here today," he said, trying to make it sound light, and failing. His good hand shook as he lighted a cigar. He regained some composure, puffing deeply to make it burn evenly.

"We'll miss you," Susan said.

"That I doubt." Oliver stood at the window, looking out at the bay and the sunlight that made every choppy wave look like a handful of coins scattered on a silver field.

"But I couldn't leave the hospital without thanking you for all you've done for me." He was speaking slowly, his good hand a fist on the window facing. His side was to Susan, and he kept his face turned slightly away, so that what she saw was the strong line of jutting jaw and the pepper-and-salt thickness of his cropped hair.

"It would seem to me that it's the other way around," she said.

"Perhaps—perhaps not," was Cox's enigmatic reply. "Those stupid fools at the Welfare Board—well . . ." He checked himself, seeing Susan's face.

"What I wanted to ask you was this." The words came in a rush. "I don't want to offer you the baby as a bribe, Susan, but if you could—would—marry me, I'd be mighty good to you both." The proud back was turned to Susan now, a rigid question mark. He added, while Susan sat speechless, "Of course you know it isn't just for the baby. I put it badly. I never proposed marriage to anyone before. I don't know how to, now. I guess I thought—I mean, I know you know how I feel about you." He turned around now, facing her. Susan saw that the usually deadpan face was transformed with feeling.

"But, Oliver, you know that I love Arch Curtis." Susan made no effort to pull her punches; she put it to him without any cushioning.

He winced, then smiled weakly. "That's my girl. You don't flirt around any. Him likewise?"

Susan nodded mutely. Reluctantly, she got to her feet. She hated to leave Oliver like this.

"Don't you want to know about the cancer clinic?" he asked.

"Well, right now it's less than the most important thing in the world to me." Susan smiled shakily. "I guess I just forgot about the cancer clinic for the moment."

"That's the nicest thing you ever said to me," Oliver told her. He began walking back and forth, his lame arm held close to his chest. "I'm no welsher. I know I made the endowment—what did that Irishman say?—contingent upon the boy, upon his being where you and he would be kind of wrapped up in one package, in case you couldn't answer me right away. Trouble is, things don't always turn out like a person plans. You answered, all right. And so did the Welfare Board." Oliver stopped to put his cigar down on an ash tray beside the bed. The sun, behind the clouds since daylight, emerged suddenly and flooded the room with light.

His struggle to express himself was an almost visible one. "If I should have learned anything at all, all these years in the school of hard knocks, it's that strings tied to presents are no good. And I didn't mean to try to buy you with the clinic—nor the baby. Only with the way I feel about you." The intense black look was one that Susan would never forget.

"The clinic trust fund has been set up, waiting, in the bank here. Today I shall arrange that any mention of Pat be taken out of it. I won't tack onto it anything about your working there. I know, now, you would want to do that yourself. You've taught me a lot, Susan." He smiled wryly. "But Palm City will have its cancer facility. The boys will like knowing it's here."

Susan swallowed with difficulty. She knew that she was saying goodbye to a man whose principles and kindliness were a giant's own. As usual, Cox made it easier for her.

"Get on with you. I hate goodbyes. I'll be around every now and then, looking in on Barney, spelling Alice at mealtimes or whenever. What are you waiting for?" The black eyes glinted with something suspiciously like moisture.

Appalled, Susan went.

CHAPTER XVIII

Grace's scholarship, while not large, was enough to be of help to the slender Farley resources.

"I can tutor three or four repeaters at the elementary level, and it will help me and them, too," she told Susan. They had adopted the shaded end of the porch, Grace usually stretched out on the newly covered couch, and Susan sitting in the swing. This afternoon, she was basting a hem in a cornflower-blue skirt. Its featherweight wool fabric was hot as she sewed, but in only a few weeks the stormy season, with its gales and sustained rains, would be upon them. And when the northeasters began, the shop windows inevitably filled with fall clothes.

"What kind of a top will you wear with that?" Grace fanned herself with the newspaper she'd been reading.

"At first, one of those cardigan things that are loose at the waist. I've got the material, a polished cotton. It looked sort of chopped off in the picture," Susan said dubiously.

"It won't look chopped off on you," Grace said comfortingly. There was silence for a few moments. Susan dropped the scissors, and Grace rolled over on her face and reached a languid arm toward the floor for them. She put them firmly on an end table near the swing.

"That's the third time. Signal for a new resting place," she pronounced. "Has Mavis called today?"

"Not since I got home from the hospital," Susan answered, biting off a thread. "She's boning up on some of the foundation subjects she'll need in her classes. She's taking her new life very seriously." Susan squinted her eyes to thread the needle.

"What about Mr. Cox?" Grace tried to sound casual.

"What about him?" Susan took a few stitches in the hem. "You sound like Arch. Oliver's a wonderful person. I like him and I respect him, but I don't love him. I might add, I miss him. It certainly was a place where things happened, Second, East, while he was there."

"He sounds like a TV star—strong and silent and suffering." Grace sighed at the romantic vision she'd dreamed up.

Susan replied mildly that while Cox had suffered with his fracture, it had been his lack of silence that had gotten him into trouble, by his own admission. "And don't get any ideas about him," she told her sister. "He's gone back to his own environment, and now that he's adjusted himself to the idea of marriage, I bet we'll be getting a wedding invitation almost any day. He'll find someone far more able to appreciate his good qualities than I. Someone who'll be a real mother to the 'hospital's baby,'" she added speculatively.

"Well, Arch seems so—so homefolksy, by comparison," Grace complained.

"You think that's not a good quality in a husband?" Susan was amused.

"Oh, I guess so. Only—wouldn't you think he'd get a crew cut, or something? That lock of hair always falling onto his forehead—"

"I told him last night he needed a haircut," Susan recalled. "Even offered to shear his neckline with the surgical scissors I was taking out of the sterilizer, when he grumbled about there not being enough hours in the day."

"How long is Dr. Hubbard going to be here?"

"Not long, now that they've got the staff pretty well set up for the start of their cancer work. And the blueprints for the new wing are divine . . ." Susan's blue eyes were starry.

The telephone rang inside, and John Farley answered it. He came to the door, the examination papers he was grading in his hand. He was well enough to undertake some of this paper work at home, and the task had made him happier.

"For you, Susan," he said.

"Arch?" Susan spilled her sewing in her quick rise from the swing.

"The hospital," her father answered, already on the way back to his desk.

"Farley?" The voice was Ma Maggie's. She sounded more clipped than usual.

"Yes?"

"Dr. Curtis says he knows you've already had a hard day, but could you come over to fourth-floor Surgery right away?"

"Yes, indeed," Susan said, wasting no words. She hung up.

"Again?" Grace was rebellious. She would have to cook dinner, and it was Susan's week in the kitchen.

"Never mind, lamb; I'll take a day when it's your week,"

Susan promised, already on her way out. She had swiftly replaced her cotton duster with a button-down-the-front uniform, and pushed her feet into white strollers.

If work holds out for this family as it has during the past few weeks, Susan thought, coaxing the old car along, *I'll be able to afford one of those gas-miser little cars for myself.* Things were looking much better for the Farleys. *But it's been rough,* Susan thought, remembering. *And the roughest of all was feeling like an outcast, while Dr. Mitchell was mad with me.* She wondered how much Mavis had had to do in bringing about such a complete change in the Chief of Staff.

She was in the elevator when she remembered that she had failed to punch in on her time card. With resigned self-discipline, she went back and did so. She had to learn to be one of a team.

Susan donned her green gown, mask and cap. As late in the day as this, there would be little activity in Surgery. Arch would no doubt have it to himself. Her glance at the other operating rooms confirmed this. They were scrubbed and sterile appearing, silent and empty.

She pushed open the heavy door. Arch was gowned and ready. He was tying on his mask when she came in.

"Hated to bother you, Susan," his brown eyes smiled their welcome and appreciation, "but this patient especially requested that you be here." Susan glanced at the inert body on the guerney beside the operating table. She gasped. It was Christopher Mitchell. His handsome face was masklike in its anesthetized sleep. His pallor made the skin cancer on his nose stand out in an ugly, scaly blotch.

"Isn't this rather sudden?" Susan's brows came together in a worried frown.

"He wanted to get this over with before Dr. Hubbard left," Arch said. "The biopsy showed basal carcinoma cells, and he'll need a graft."

"Goodness, is Hubbard going to do it?" Susan's eyes were big.

"No. I am." Arch was obviously proud. But his eyes were humble, too, Susan saw. "Hubbard is going to assist. How about that?" His wide mouth grinned.

"Oh, brother!" Susan was going to ask if Arch knew how far advanced the growth was, when the great cancer specialist came in. He apologized for being late, explaining that his plane was leaving at midnight, and there had been much to do.

"I don't like to hurry like this," he grumbled. "Getting too old to move this fast. It gets more and more difficult to leave haste outside the white line." He referred to the demarcation line denoting the sterile boundary outside the operating-room wing. "But I recognized the fact that if Dr. Mitchell had not done this on impulse, the doing would be put off. And that makes our work harder."

As he talked, he was readying himself. By the time he was prepared, only his spectacled eyes showing between mask and the green skull cap, Dr. Mitchell was on the table and the straps adjusted.

"If you can't keep out of the way of the nose surgery," Arch was saying to the anesthesiologist, "be prepared to use a tube into the lungs." The man nodded.

Susan, the spread of instruments ready, stood by, waiting for Arch's go ahead. It came, sharp and clipped.

"Scalpel," he said, bent low over the diaphragm, the skin just below the rib cage clean and free of any follicles of hair.

"From here, I think," he said, directing a look of inquiry upward and sideways to Dr. Hubbard. The great man nodded. Haste had vanished from the atmosphere. Arch's words were deliberate, calculation implicit in every syllable and movement.

"Merthiolate, here to here," Arch told Susan, who daubed on the pinkish-red antiseptic.

The nurse with the blood-pressure cuff made a quiet answer to Dr. Hubbard's questioning look. He nodded with satisfaction.

Arch cut a section of top flesh from the Chief's lean barrel wall, about an inch-and-a-half square. Susan handed the prearranged bandaging to Dr. Hubbard, who manipulated it with deft hands. They weren't going to sew this up, preferring that nature do its resurfacing by its own extension of cell-growth. The doctor would always have a scar there, but it would heal cleanly, this way.

Arch had gone around to the patient's head. His skilled fingers excised the diseased surface. The tissue was damaged throughout the area of the radium scar. He talked as he worked, as was his custom. Susan wondered, fleetingly, if he would talk if operating alone, with no one to listen. Arch had told her once that it helped him to think clearly. "The cartilage is affected," she heard him say.

She drew in a sharp breath. That meant Dr. Chris would

lack symmetry in the nose. Arch was still talking, his baritone voice clear and assured. Susan, perhaps more than anyone else, understood why Christopher Mitchell had wanted this unknown resident to do such a ticklish job. Arch had prepared himself as thoroughly as was humanly possible. To him, every surgical procedure was a major one, a life-and-death procedure. This was one of the things he'd emphasized to Susan in their post-operative coffee sessions. "Because no matter how minor, when you cut into human flesh, the consequences can be major," he insisted.

Dr. Hubbard was handing Arch the graft. Working quickly, he affixed the square of skin to Dr. Mitchell's nose. There was a lot of bleeding. Arch muttered, "Take care lest it float." Long since, the tube had been inserted to administer the gas directly into the lungs. Undoubtedly, the doctor-patient had swallowed a lot of blood.

The dressing was being applied. It looked like a giant burlesque of a nose. Susan wondered nervously if the dressing would stay in place; it protruded a good twelve inches from Dr. Mitchell's face.

"He's going to be pretty sick," Arch told Susan when the patient had been wheeled into the Recovery Room. "Is Amy on a case?" he asked, taking off the bloodstained gown with an appearance of utter weariness. Dr. Hubbard had made hurried farewells, a brusque congratulation of the younger surgeon, and hustled out. He'd been as sure as humanly possible that by cutting the necessary fraction of an inch farther than the cancer apparently grew they had removed the questionable area.

Susan didn't know about Amy. Vaguely, she thought her friend was on vacation. A quick call to Mrs. Branch confirmed this.

Susan and Arch went upstairs together. Mavis was waiting in the uncomfortable so-called lounge the hospital provided for relatives of patients in Surgery.

She had cropped all her black curls close to her head. And the result was to make her look very young and vulnerable. Susan smiled at her.

Arch spoke first. "He feels pretty bad right now, and will all night," he told Mavis, his voice full of sympathy.

"Did you get it all?"

Arch lifted his shoulders. "As nearly as we could tell. I'm sure we did. But he isn't going to be as handsome," he said regretfully.

Mavis sat down abruptly. It had been a long two hours.

"Like always, there's no nurse on the register," Susan reported.

"He'll be down in twenty minutes or so," Arch said. "He's reacting now. Spoke to me, as a matter of fact. Like Mavis, he wanted to know if we got it all. I doubt he'll remember my telling him to keep his nose clean." Arch grinned. Then he sobered. "We'd better go have coffee and something to eat, while he's still upstairs." Susan realized that Arch expected to stand by.

Mavis looked quickly at him, then nodded her agreement. "I'm staying," she said.

Arch looked at her approvingly, then at Susan. He raised an eyebrow. "She'll make a pretty good nurse, don't you think?" he asked.

Susan showed her dimple. Once, such open approval of Mavis Pennington would have hurt her. Not any more. She took the smaller girl's arm close in her own. Her look met Arch's, on the other side of Mavis.

"You're both mighty good to me," Mavis murmured gratefully. "And to Uncle Chris." They got on the elevator together. "You make a good cancer-combat team, the three of you. St. Patrick's is going to be famous someday. But I'll tell you one thing." She got off the elevator ahead of them, and shoved them together as they, too, emerged. "You can just move over. There'll be two of the Mitchell clan, as well as two Curtis experts, in the new cancer clinic."

Susan and Arch laughed at her intensity, then their looks held. Susan, in a rush of happiness, realized what a fruitful summer it had been, after all, at St. Patrick's. It wasn't only the big, sprawling hospital that was growing. Somehow, it impelled them all to grow along with it.

Susan felt it had been a long time ago that she'd been the new nurse on Second, East.

But it was Arch who voiced their feeling.

"Move over," he repeated thoughtfully. "In this business, you do that more than in any other one. There's always room for another, and another. And if you move right, you move up. Come on, you two." He shepherded them ahead of him, into the cafeteria.